Dawn's Wicked Stepsister

**Look for these and other books
in the Baby-sitters Club series:**

1 Kristy's Great Idea

2 Claudia and the
     Phantom Phone Calls

3 The Truth About Stacey

4 Mary Anne Saves the Day

5 Dawn and the
     Impossible Three

6 Kristy's Big Day

7 Claudia and Mean Janine

8 Boy-Crazy Stacey

9 The Ghost at Dawn's House

#10 Logan Likes Mary Anne!

#11 Kristy and the Snobs

#12 Claudia and the New Girl

#13 Good-bye Stacey, Good-bye

#14 Hello, Mallory

#15 Little Miss Stoneybrook
     . . . and Dawn

#16 Jessi's Secret Language

#17 Mary Anne's
     Bad-Luck Mystery

#18 Stacey's Mistake

#19 Claudia and the Bad Joke

#20 Kristy and the
     Walking Disaster

#21 Mallory and the
     Trouble With Twins

#22 Jessi Ramsey, Pet-sitter

#23 Dawn on the Coast

#24 Kristy and the
     Mother's Day Surprise

#25 Mary Anne and the
     Search for Tigger

#26 Claudia and the
     Sad Good-bye

#27 Jessi and the Superbrat

#28 Welcome Back, Stacey!

#29 Mallory and the
     Mystery Diary

#30 Mary Anne and the
     Great Romance

#31 Dawn's Wicked Stepsister

#32 Kristy and the
     Secret of Susan

Super Specials:

1 Baby-sitters on Board!

2 Baby-sitters'
     Summer Vacation

3 Baby-sitters'
     Winter Vacation

Dawn's Wicked Stepsister
Ann M. Martin

AN
APPLE
PAPERBACK

SCHOLASTIC INC.
New York Toronto London Auckland Sydney

*This book is for
all my friends at
PS 2.*

Cover art by Hodges Soileau

ISBN 0-590-42497-1

12 11 10 9   2 3 4 5/9

Printed in the U.S.A.   40

First Scholastic printing, February 1990

CHAPTER 1

Mom's wedding bouquet was flying through the air. Mary Anne, my new stepsister, and I were both leaping for it. At the last second, Mary Anne's arms seemed to grow about five inches, and even though she is not terribly coordinated, she *caught* the *bouquet*.

I couldn't believe it.

The bouquet was my mother's. *I* should have caught it. Well, that wasn't quite true. I don't know of any rule that says a daughter should catch her mom's bouquet. Plus, there were several people behind Mary Anne and me — several other women who wanted to catch it, too — and we were all supposed to have an equal shot at it. Why did we want to catch it so badly? Because there's this belief that if an unmarried woman catches the bride's bouquet after the bride has tossed it, that

1

woman will be the next to get married.

Now Mary Anne and I are only thirteen, so we didn't have any plans to get married, but I *still* thought I should have caught my own mother's bouquet. Anyway, I guess Mary Anne just tried a little harder than I did. After all, she's got a boyfriend. Logan Bruno. Maybe she hopes they'll get married someday, when they're older and ready for it.

Anyway, Mary Anne was holding the bouquet triumphantly over her head. "I caught it!" she said with a gasp.

Well, of course she'd caught it. She'd practically killed the rest of us in the process. I don't know why she was so surprised.

Everyone was laughing and cheering.

"All right, Mary *Anne!*" called Kristy Thomas, one of her best friends.

I got into the spirit of things. Mary Anne is shy — extremely shy. And she's one of the nicest people I know. She's my best friend, she's now my stepsister, and she *does* have a boyfriend, while I don't. So I didn't mind *too* much that she'd caught the bouquet. I found myself turning to her and giving her a big hug.

"Congratulations . . . sis!" I said.

Mary Anne, the world's teariest person alive, immediately began to cry.

"Sis," she repeated. "It's really true. We're stepsisters now."

"No, just sisters," I corrected her.

Mary Anne's tears flowed harder. "Thanks . . . sis," she replied.

It was my mother's wedding day. Well, it was her second wedding day. Her first one had been sixteen years ago, when she married my father. About fourteen years later they had gotten divorced. We were living in California then — Mom; Dad; my younger brother, Jeff; and I. After the divorce, Mom moved Jeff and me here to Stoneybrook, Connecticut. She didn't choose Stoneybrook randomly. Stoneybrook is the town where she grew up, and her parents, my grandparents, were still living here. It was also the town where she had gone to school with a guy she liked a lot (although that didn't have anything to do with her decision to move back here). The guy's name was Richard Spier, and he is Mary Anne's father. She and Mr. Sp — I mean, Richard (Mary Anne and I had decided to call our stepparents by their first names, Richard and Sharon) had dated when they were in high school. But my grandparents hadn't approved of Richard. Mom's family had a lot of money;

3

Richard's didn't. They said he came from the wrong side of the tracks. What soreheads. And they saw to it that after graduation, their daughter (my mother) got as far away from Richard as she could. They sent her to college in California. That's where she met and married my dad. Meanwhile, back here in Connecticut, Richard met and married Mary Anne's mom. He put himself through law school and got a good job (fake out on my grandparents), even though some terrible things happened. His parents died, Mary Anne's mother's parents died — and Mary Anne's *mom* died. It was awful. Mary Anne was quite young when she lost her mother and barely remembers her. Still, I think it must have been terrible to be almost alone in the world, just Richard and Mary Anne.

But fate intervened. (I read that sentence in a book once. Isn't it great?) Mom and Jeff and I moved back here, and in no time, Mary Anne and I not only met and became friends, but figured out that our parents had been in love years ago. We reintroduced them and — zap! They started dating and today they'd gotten married. Finally. Sometimes I wonder what would have happened if they'd gotten married after high school. For one thing, Mary Anne

4

and Jeff and I wouldn't be here, at least not in these particular bodies. That was a weird thought.

I guess you probably want to know a little about the wedding. Well, since it was the second one for both Mom and Richard, they'd kept it simple and small. Mom didn't even wear a wedding gown, just a gorgeous new dress. They got married in the chapel of a local church and didn't have any attendants. (Mary Anne and I were awfully disappointed. We'd wanted to be bridesmaids.) The guests were three friends of my brother's (the Pike triplets), Mary Anne's and my friends from the Baby-sitters Club (I'll tell you more about the BSC later), some work friends of Mom's and Richard's, and my grandparents. Mary Anne's and my friends (just so you know) were: Kristy Thomas, Stacey McGill, Jessi Ramsey, Mallory Pike (she's the triplets' sister), Claudia Kishi, and Logan Bruno. Even though the wedding ceremony was short, it was pretty traditional. There were flowers at the altar, Mom and Richard said vows and exchanged rings, Richard kissed my mother on the lips in front of absolutely everybody, and Mom even wore something old, something new, something borrowed, and something blue.

Now we were at this *très* swank French restaurant called Chez Maurice. "We" is all the people I just told you about. We had had a sumptuous dinner (actually it was lunch, and I had had trouble finding a good vegetarian dish on the menu — Mom and Jeff and I are health nuts), my mother had just tossed her bouquet (standing backward on her chair and throwing it over her shoulder), and Mary Anne had just caught it.

I was trying to be happy for Mary Anne, but the truth is, I would gladly have killed to get my hands on that bouquet.

Luckily, I was distracted from those thoughts. The wedding reception was over and people were starting to leave. First Mom's and Richard's friends left. Then my grandparents left. Then Mr. Pike arrived to pick up the triplets and Jeff. Jeff was going to spend the night at the Pikes' house. He could have spent the night with our grandparents, but he was just dying to visit with the triplets. (I think I forgot to tell you that Jeff lives in California with our father now. He moved back there because he simply couldn't adjust to Connecticut.)

Meanwhile, Mom and my new stepfather were going to the Strathmoore Inn for the shortest honeymoon on record — they were going to be back the next day. And that day, Sunday, was moving day. Mary Anne, her father, and her kitten, Tigger, were moving into our house, which is bigger than theirs.

" 'Bye, Jeff!" I called as the Pikes drove off. "See you tomorrow!"

" 'Bye, Dawn!" he replied.

A few moments later Charlie Thomas, Kristy's oldest brother, arrived in his beat-up second-hand car to take Mary Anne, all of our friends, and me back to Mary Anne's house. We were going to sit around and dish about the wedding for awhile. ("Dish" means "gossip.") Then Mary Anne and I were going to spend one last night in Mary Anne's room at her old house — by ourselves. Mary Anne was nostalgic. I was excited and nervous. I'm not used to sleeping in a house without any adults around.

As my friends and I climbed into Charlie's car, I waved to Richard and the new Mrs. Spier. That's right — Mom was changing her name. She said she wanted to take on the name of her husband. Why? It's beyond me. I wanted the name I'd been born with, which is Dawn Schafer. Mom said it was perfectly all right for Jeff and me to keep our old names.

"Is everybody in?" called Charlie, glancing in the rearview mirror.

"Yes," chorused the eight of us. We sure were in. We were *squished* in, like sardines in a can.

We were pretty quiet as we drove over to Mary Anne's. But as soon as Charlie let us out and we'd settled ourselves on the floor in the Spiers' living room, we all began talking at once.

The first thing Kristy said was, "Ew! Your parents kissed in public! PDA! PDA! Public Display of Affection!"

Mary Anne blushed to the roots of her hair.

Then Claudia said, "Mary Anne, I can't believe you cried so much at the wedding that all your makeup came off."

Mary Anne blushed an even brighter red.

Everyone started laughing.

I looked around at my friends. I felt happy. I felt happier than happy. My mom had gotten married again, and I had a new stepfather and a new stepsister.

I smiled at everyone — Kristy, Claudia, Logan, Stacey, Mal, Jessi, and Mary Anne. . . .

CHAPTER 2

I was lucky to have such a nice group of friends, and I wouldn't have had them at all if it weren't for Mary Anne. She was one of the first people I met after I moved to Stoneybrook. And she introduced me to her friends in the Baby-sitters Club. The BSC is a business that Kristy started. We baby-sit for families in our neighborhoods. But the club members aren't just business partners, they're friends, too. And, boy, am I grateful for them. They made moving across country and switching to a new school in the middle of the year a lot easier than I'd expected. Plus, they're very different people (I mean, from each other), and I like that. They aren't a clique of girls who have to dress alike, talk alike, think alike, and be sure to have a boyfriend at all times.

Take Kristy Thomas, for instance. She's the president of the BSC. Kristy is an ideas person.

She thought up the club and got it going. She's an extrovert who can be bossy and has sort of a big mouth. She's also a tomboy who loves sports. She likes kids, too, of course. (We all do, or we wouldn't enjoy baby-sitting so much.) Kristy likes sports and children so much that she organized a softball team for kids who are too young to try out for Little League, or who are afraid to try out for it.

Kristy couldn't care less about the way she dresses or whether she has a boyfriend. She thinks planning outfits and putting on makeup and jewelry are a waste of time. So she almost always wears the same kinds of clothes — jeans, a turtleneck shirt, a sweater (in the winter), running shoes, and sometimes this baseball cap with a collie on it. Kristy has brown hair and eyes, and is the shortest kid in our class.

Kristy's family life is complicated — even more complicated than mine. Her father left her family not long after David Michael, her little brother, was born. He just up and left. So Mrs. Thomas pulled herself together and raised Kristy, David Michael, and Sam and Charlie (they're Kristy's big brothers, who go to high school) on her own. She got a good job and held everything in place. Then, a couple of years ago, she met Watson Brewer, this divorced, balding millionaire with two little kids, Karen and Andrew. Karen is almost seven now, and Andrew is almost five. At first, Kristy hated the idea of Watson. She didn't want a stepfamily. But she didn't have any choice in the matter. Her mom and Watson were in love, and the summer after we finished seventh grade, they got married. Then, just like with Mary Anne and me, Kristy's family moved across town to Watson's house. Actually, it's a mansion, which is why they moved into it. It's huge and has room for everyone — including Karen and Andrew, who live there two weekends each month . . . and Emily Michelle, the two-year-old Vietnamese girl the Brewers adopted! Plus Nannie, Kristy's grandmother, who moved in to help take care of Emily and the other kids. Kristy's house is like a zoo, especially considering that Shannon and Boo-Boo live there, too. Shannon is David Michael's puppy, and Boo-Boo is Watson's fat, old, mean cat. Considering that Kristy used to live a quiet life next door to Mary Anne and across the street from Claudia Kishi (the three of them grew up together), I'd say she's adapted to her new life pretty well.

The club vice-president is Claudia Kishi. If

ever two people were opposites, it's Kristy and Claudia. Claud has no interest in sports. What she likes is art, and she is *good* at it. She can paint, draw, sculpt, make jewelry, you name it. She's got art supplies jamming up her room. They're everywhere — in boxes, in her closet, under her bed. And that's not the only stuff cluttering up her room. There are also Nancy Drew books and junk food. The Nancy Drew books are hidden because her parents think she should be reading classics and things. But Claud is just not a good student — even though she's very smart. What a shame that her older sister, Janine, is an actual genius. If you ask me, Mr. and Mrs. Kishi should be glad Claud is reading anything at all. Oh, and the junk food is hidden because Claud's parents don't approve of that, either, but Claud can't live without it. She's got Ring-Dings, Ho-Hos, Yodels, potato chips, gum, and other stuff in every nook and cranny.

It's a good thing Claud is one of those lucky people who never seems to get overweight or pimply from so much bad food. If she did, that would be a dead giveaway to her parents that she's hiding food. Luckily, Claudia is slender and absolutely gorgeous. She's Japanese-American and has long silky, black hair, dark almond-shaped eyes, and a creamy complexion.

And her clothes! Nobody dresses like Claudia. She is totally cool. She wears funky stuff like pink sparkly high-topped sneakers, or short flared skirts over skintight leggings, or wild jewelry she's made herself. She's good at pottery and is always creating earrings (she has one hole in one ear and two in the other) or beaded necklaces or bracelets. Claudia has had several boyfriends, including a long-distance one named Will, but she doesn't have a special one right now.

Claud lives with her parents and Janine, but no pets. Her grandmother Mimi used to live with the Kishis, but Mimi died not long ago. Everyone was sad about that. Claudia and Mimi had been very close.

My new stepsister, Mary Anne, is the club secretary and you already know some things about her. For instance, you know she's shy, cries and gets embarrassed easily, and that her family and mine are in the process of becoming one. She has no brothers or sisters, but she's got her kitten, Tigger. And she's the only one of us BSC members to have a true boyfriend.

Some things you don't know about Mary Anne are how sensitive she is and what a good listener she is. Kids often go to Mary Anne for advice. She always takes people seriously. She has a good sense of humor, but she never laughs *at* people, like when they trip or make a mistake or something.

Before Mary Anne's father met my mother, he'd brought his daughter up quite strictly. He had invented these rules for her. For instance, Richard picked out Mary Anne's clothes for her, made her wear her hair in braids, and do (or not do) all these other things. It was his way of trying to be a good father *and* a good mother. But when he loosened up, he saw that Mary Anne was still going to be a good kid. She did start dressing differently, and she wears her brown hair loose now, but otherwise she hasn't changed much. Can you believe that she and Kristy are best friends? (I mean, I'm her other best friend, but she and Kristy have been best friends practically since birth.) They are *so* different. Kristy is a loudmouth and Mary Anne is quiet and shy — and hates sports. Instead, she likes sewing and knitting and stuff. Still, they're best friends.

I know our parents' marriage is a little difficult on Mary Anne. After all, Mary Anne is leaving the neighborhood she was born in (I wonder who will move into her house), and joining a family that's pretty different from hers. Mom and I are fairly laid-back. Even so, Mary Anne and I are looking forward to being sisters. We've even decided to share my room, despite the fact that the guest room could be Mary Anne's bedroom. We just know we're going to be great sisters.

Okay, on to Stacey McGill, our treasurer. Stacey and Claud are best friends and very much alike in some ways — but very different in others. They're alike in that they share a taste for wild clothes and jewelry, and they're both sophisticated and have sometimes-boy-friends. Stacey even has a body wave in her blonde hair, and pierced ears like Claudia's. Plus, she *comes from New York City*. Stacey, who is an only child, grew up there and lived in the city until her father's company transferred him to Connecticut. That was just before.seventh grade. Stacey had lived here for about a year when the company transferred Mr. McGill *back* to New York. Then, Stacey had been *there* for *less* than a year when her parents decided to divorce. Her father wanted to stay in New York with his job, but her mother wanted to return to Stoneybrook. Stacey's parents said she could live with either one of them. It was a tough choice, but she finally returned to Connecticut and the BSC. She visits her father in New York a lot, though.

Life has not been easy for Stacey, as you can see. Apart from everything else, she has diabetes. That's a disease in which her pancreas doesn't control the level of sugar in her blood properly so Stacey has to do it herself with daily injections (yuck) of something called insulin, and by sticking to a strict diet. NO SWEETS. If Stacey doesn't do these things, she could get *really* sick. I mean, she could go into a diabetic coma. So far, she has taken very good care of herself. I like Stacey a lot. She is funny, and not at all stuck-up.

Well, I'm the club's alternate officer. (I'll explain that later.) You know an awful lot about me already. Let's see. What don't you know? I have extra long, extra blonde hair (it's almost white), and very pale blue eyes. I love mysteries, especially ghost stories, so I'm perfectly happy to be living in a centuries-old farmhouse with a *secret passage* in it that just might be haunted. I hate cold weather and love warm weather. Like Jeff and my parents, I *adore* health food and can't stand junk food. Some people think I'm weird, but I don't care —

16

much. I like to think I'm an individual. I do what I want (unless it's going to hurt someone), I eat what I want, and I dress the way I want — a style my friends call California casual. I guess that style falls somewhere between Stacey's and Kristy's. Here's something you should know about my mom — she's totally scatterbrained, and she is *not* a good housekeeper. She's like the absentminded professor in that old movie.

Then there are Jessi Ramsey and Mallory Pike, junior officers in the club. Jessi and Mal are best friends. They're also sixth-graders, while the rest of us are eighth-graders. We all go to Stoneybrook Middle School. Mal and Jessi are both the oldest kids in their families, both love horses, both love to read, both think their parents treat them like infants — even though recently they were allowed to get their ears pierced (just one hole in each ear, of course) — and neither one of them has ever had a boyfriend.

But the similarities end there. Mal comes from a huge family (she has seven younger brothers and sisters), while Jessi comes from an average-sized family — one younger sister and a baby brother. Mal wants to be an author and illustrator of children's books when she grows up and is always writing in her private journal, while Jessi is thinking of becoming a professional ballet dancer. She takes lessons at a special dance school in Stamford and has even *starred* in some ballet productions. One last difference: Mal is white; Jessi is black. Jessi's skin color doesn't matter a bit to any of *us*, but it sure mattered to some people in Stoneybrook when the Ramseys first moved here. They gave Jessi and her family a really hard time. See, there are hardly any other blacks in Stoneybrook (Jessi is the only black student in the sixth grade), and some people wanted to keep it that way. They were downright mean to the Ramseys, but things have cooled off, thank goodness.

The last person who was over at Mary Anne's on that sunny day after the wedding was Logan Bruno. He's only sort of a member of the Baby-sitters Club, but since he's Mary Anne's boyfriend, he was invited to dish about the wedding with the rest of us. All us girls like Logan — but no one except Mary Anne likes him in that special way.

Logan is funny and kind. He enjoys sports. He cares very much about Mary Anne and

18

doesn't mind when she's feeling extra shy. And he is drop-dead gorgeous. He looks like a movie star.

Logan's family is from Louisville, Kentucky. They moved here just before we began eighth grade. Logan has a younger sister and a younger brother. His family speaks with a southern accent. Logan says "Luevulle" for "Louisville" and "mah hayer" for "my hair." What's funny (sort of) is that his little brother, Hunter, has allergies, so *he* says "bah hayer" for "my hair" because his nose (doze) is always stuffed up!

The eight of us dished for about two hours. Then everyone began to leave.

"Gotta go, you guys," said Logan, standing up. "I'm sitting at the Rodowskys' tonight."

"Charlie's going to be here to pick me up any second," said Kristy.

Before we knew it, Mary Anne and I were alone. We'd been looking forward to ordering in a pizza for dinner and watching a scary movie on TV, but now I could tell that we both felt sort of empty. Our parents were away, and Mary Anne was about to spend her last night ever in her old room. And it didn't even look like her room anymore, since it was half packed up. We tried to make the best of things, though.

But I knew we were thinking about the next day, and wondering what, exactly, it would bring.

CHAPTER 3

Moving day!

Mary Anne and I woke up early that morning. To tell you the truth, we hadn't gotten much sleep the night before. Every time we heard the teensiest sound we were sure a robber was breaking into the house. You might think that I wouldn't mind odd sounds, since I like mysteries and sleep in a room with a hidden entrance to a secret passage in the wall — but my mother is always home at night. It's different when no adults are around. My mother probably couldn't get the better of either a robber or a ghost, but I always feel comforted knowing she's in the next room.

"Boy," said Mary Anne at 3:15 A.M., when we'd been awakened for about the thirtieth time, "you should have been living in Stoneybrook when Kristy, Claudia, Stacey, and I thought we were being harassed by a phantom phone caller."

"A phantom phone caller?" I repeated.

"Yeah. There was this guy who would call people's houses at night. If no one answered the phone, he'd come rob the house. The Baby-sitters Club was brand-new then, and us club members were scared to death. We were sure he was going to call sometime when one of us was sitting, figure out that no adults were around, and then come rob the house with *us in* it!"

"What did you do?" I whispered.

"Lots of things. One night I was sitting for David Michael because he had a cold, and Kristy and the rest of her family were out — probably visiting Watson, I don't remember. Anyway, I rigged up all these burglar alarms — and kept setting them off by accident. Once *Louie* set one off. Remember Louie? The Thomases' old collie? Anyway, that seemed like a really scary time, but when I think of it now, it's kind of funny."

I giggled. Mary Anne and I felt better for about five minutes. Then we heard a *c-r-e-a-k* and we both shrieked.

Were we ever glad when Mom and Richard pulled up in front of the house at ten o'clock that morning. They'd already picked up Jeff.

Mary Anne and I flew out the front door. "Hi! Hi!" we called.

"What a nice, warm welcome," said Mom.

If she only knew. We were really just relieved.

"Well, now what?" I asked.

"Now we wait for the moving van," said Richard. "It should be here in a minute."

The five of us stood around on the Spiers' front lawn.

Richard tried to make conversation. "Jeff had a fine time at the Pikes' last night, didn't you, Jeff?" he said.

"Yes, sir," Jeff replied. (He would have to work on that "sir" business. Or maybe not. He was going back to California the next night.)

"Did you girls have fun?" Mom asked us.

Mary Anne and I glanced at each other. "Sort of," I replied.

Across the street, the door to the Kishis' house opened and Claud dashed across her lawn and over to us.

"I can't believe you're *moving*," she said fervently to Mary Anne. "Oh, hi, Mr. Spier. Hi, Mrs. Scha — Mrs. Spier." Claud rushed on. "You and Kristy always lived across the street from me. Then Kristy left, and now you're leaving, Mary Anne. The triangle is completely broken up."

Now why did Claud have to go and say that? Of course, Mary Anne started to cry. To make things worse, the moving van arrived then. It pulled into the Spiers' driveway.

Mary Anne's tears fell faster. "I don't want to leave," she said. "I've never lived anywhere but here."

I began to feel guilty. Why? Because underneath the guilt I was excited. I couldn't wait for my new sister and father to get settled at our house. And I knew the only way that would happen was by making Mary Anne miserable. I didn't have much patience for her tears.

"Come on, sis," I said to her. "You know it's going to be great. We've both always wanted a sister."

Mary Anne watched the movers carry her dresser through the front door and load it into the van.

"Sis?" said Claudia.

We barely heard her. "There's my dresser," said Mary Anne. "It won't even fit in your — I mean, our — room. I'll have to put it in the guest room. Who ever heard of sleeping in one room and keeping your dresser in another?"

"But the rest of your clothes will hang in my closet," I told her. "We made room, remember?"

"Of course I remember," snapped Mary Anne. "I'm not stupid."

Well, obviously Mary Anne wasn't in as good a mood as I was. She must be one of those people who gets crabby if she doesn't have enough sleep.

She and Claud and Jeff and I stood on the lawn and watched the movers. Mary Anne's eyes misted up as each item came out of her house — even stupid things, like boxes marked CLEANING SUPPLIES.

And she wasn't cheered when neighbors started dropping over with good-bye presents. First Mrs. Kishi came by with a casserole.

"I don't think you'll be doing much cooking today," she said.

Mary Anne cried.

Then Stacey and Mal (whose houses are back to back) came over with brownies they'd baked together.

Mary Anne sobbed.

Then Myriah and Gabbie Perkins, who had

moved into Kristy's old house next door, came over with a bunch of flowers they'd picked.

Mary Anne became a gusher.

I was relieved when the van was finally loaded, we'd said our good-byes, and my new family had climbed into the Spiers' car and followed the van to my house. I thought Mary Anne would cheer up once she was away from *her* house.

But, *no*.

She turned into the Crab Queen.

"I can't believe we gave our sofa to the Salvation Army," she said, looking around our living room, which was now on the crowded side.

"There wasn't any room for it," I pointed out. I didn't bother to add that Tigger had clawed it and the stuffing was coming out. It was awful-looking. Why would we want it?

Later, Mary Anne and I went upstairs to our bedroom. It now held two beds, two desks, and an extra bookcase, plus several cartons of Mary Anne's possessions. Originally, we'd thought we could fit her dresser in the room, too, but as I already said, we couldn't. The room was just too crowded. It looked like a furniture warehouse. We kept tripping over things.

"I'm sure it'll seem better when your boxes are unpacked," I said. "At least *they* won't take up space."

Mary Anne sort of grunted.

Just then we heard mewing.

"Oh, that's Tigger!" cried Mary Anne. "Where is he? I bet he thinks he's lost."

Mary Anne rushed into the hall, found Tigger, scooped him up, and brought him into our room. "Poor thing," she said, stroking his back. "He's all disoriented. I don't blame you a bit for crying, Tiggy." (I rolled my eyes.)

Mary Anne should never have said that. She put Tigger down and he continued to wander around the house and mew for *six hours*. I thought he (and Mary Anne) would drive my mother insane.

They nearly drove the movers insane, too. Mary Anne kept jumping around them, exclaiming, "There's Tigger! Don't step on him! Don't let him out! Don't drop that chair on him!"

The rest of the time, Mary Anne moped. She didn't unpack the cartons in our room. She wasn't even cheered up by the bouquets of flowers that kept arriving all day. Everyone wanted to congratulate us, but Mary Anne couldn't have cared less.

* * *

By Sunday, she seemed better, though. Tigger was learning his way around our house, so he stopped mewing. And Mary Anne was forced to unpack her cartons because she needed the things that were in them. When everything had been put away, Mary Anne looked around our room. "You know," she said, "this isn't half bad."

I smiled. "Hey, I've got an idea. Let's pick out our clothes for school tomorrow, only you pick out one of my outfits, and I'll pick out one of yours."

"Okay!" Mary Anne actually smiled back at me. She even said, "This is fun . . . sis."

That night, Jeff had to fly back to Los Angeles. His visit had been short, but school *was* in session and Mom and Dad didn't want him to miss too much of it.

Jeff and I always travel to L.A. at night because of the time difference. It's three hours earlier in L.A., and the flight is about five hours long. So if we put Jeff on a plane that leaves around seven, he travels (Mom thinks he sleeps) for five hours, which means he arrives in L.A. around midnight our time — but only nine o'clock California time. Jeff could get in a good night's sleep and even go to school the next day. A miracle of modern science.

All of us — Mom, Richard, Mary Anne, Jeff, and I — drove to the airport to see Jeff off. Our good-byes are usually pretty sad. But this time, Jeff seemed more concerned than sad. After he'd loaded up on comic books for the long flight, he pulled me away from everyone else.

"What is it?" I asked.

Jeff frowned. "I'm not sure. I used to like Mary Anne, but this weekend I didn't like her. And I don't think she likes us."

"Oh, come on, Jeff," I said. "She just didn't want to move."

"Well, it's going to be awhile before I come to Stoneybrook again. I think this new family is going to have some . . . trouble."

I had to admit that Jeff was right. Things hadn't gotten off to the greatest of starts. But they would improve . . . wouldn't they?

Jeff's plane was announced then, and our sad good-byes began. Jeff and Mom hugged. Jeff and I hugged. Mary Anne kissed Jeff awkwardly on the cheek. And Jeff shook Richard's hand and said, "Good-bye, sir."

Then my brother turned and walked onto the boarding ramp.

CHAPTER 4

Monday was a BSC meeting day.

Mary Anne and I showed up in our borrowed outfits, which, of course, we'd already worn to school that day. Our friends had noticed right away. And Claudia had said, "You guys are so lucky. You just doubled your wardrobes without paying a cent!"

However, neither Mary Anne nor I was in the *best* of moods by the time we got to the meeting. I had tripped over Tigger that afternoon (I had not hurt him, but Mary Anne had given me a *look*), and she had been completely grossed out when she'd opened our refrigerator and found bean sprouts in it.

"There's something *growing* in there!" she'd shrieked.

I couldn't help laughing, and Mary Anne had huffed off, mad.

Our BSC meetings always start at five-thirty

on the nose — the second that Claudia's digital clock, our official club timepiece, changes from 5:29 to five-thirty. The meetings last until six and are held three times a week, on Mondays, Wednesdays, and Fridays. We hold them late in the day in case any of us has a baby-sitting job, a class, or an appointment in the afternoon.

Before I tell you what went on at the meeting that day which, as it turned out, was the official beginning of the Pike Plague, only none of us knew that then, I'd better tell you a little about our club — how it runs and operates.

The BSC is really more a business than a club. As I mentioned earlier, Kristy thought it up. She got the idea for it way back at the beginning of seventh grade. That was before her mom had married Watson, when the Thomases still lived across the street from Claudia. In those days, Kristy, Sam, and Charlie took turns baby-sitting for David Michael after school. But, of course, a day came along when none of them was free to sit. Mrs. Thomas wasn't upset. She understood that kids have things to do. So she got on the phone to find a baby-sitter. Only that turned out to be a lot easier said than done. Kristy watched her make call after call. *Every*one seemed to be busy. And that was when Kristy got her great idea. She thought it would be wonderful if her mother (or any parent) could make just one call and reach a whole bunch of sitters at once. So she decided to form a baby-sitting business in her neighborhood. She asked Mary Anne, Claudia, and Claudia's new friend Stacey to join her. The girls decided on club meeting times when people could call them to line up a baby-sitter. With four girls at each meeting, Kristy reasoned, one of them was bound to be free. So our clients would practically be guaranteed a sitter with just one phone call. And she was right. The club has been a huge success. Now there are seven of us sitters, plus two associate club members.

How do people know when and where to reach us? Because we advertise. As I've said, Kristy is an ideas person. In order to start the club, she and her friends placed a small ad in the Stoneybrook newspaper and stuck about a million fliers in people's mailboxes. (We still distribute fliers from time to time.) They also spread the news by word of mouth. You know — just telling people what they were doing. Well, the club caught on quickly. By the time I moved to Connecticut in January, the girls needed me as a new member because they had so much business. Later, they took on two associate members — Logan, and a friend of Kristy's named Shannon Kilbourne. The associate members don't come to meetings; they're backup people we can call on in case someone needs a sitter when all us club members are busy. Believe me, that happens sometimes. Anyway, then Stacey had to move back to New York, so we replaced her with both Jessi and Mal, and then Stacey returned to Connecticut, so of course we let her right back in the club. We needed her, and besides, we would *never* have told an original member that she couldn't be part of the club anymore. The club members are like sisters (or in Logan's case, he's like our brother).

What does each club member do? Well, I'll tell you, starting with Kristy, since she's the president. As our ideas person, Kristy figured out how the club would run and is always coming up with new plans. For instance, it was Kristy who decided that we should run a playgroup for awhile last summer, and that a nice Mother's Day gift for our clients (and for some of our own mothers) would be to take their kids off their hands and give them a day of freedom and relaxation. So we took a huge bunch of kids to a carnival on the Saturday before Mother's Day. Kristy was also the one who thought up Kid-Kits. Kid-Kits are boxes (we each have one) that we decorated and then filled with our old games, books, and toys, and a few new items such as coloring books, construction paper, and Magic Markers. We bring our kits along with us on some of our sitting jobs, and the kids adore them. There's just something about playing with other people's toys. . . . Anyway, because the children like the Kid-Kits, they like us, so their *parents* like us, and they're more apt to call the BSC again. I think Kristy will become a great businesswoman one day. Kristy's job, aside from getting good ideas, is to run the meetings, which she loves doing, because she likes being in charge.

Claudia, our VP, is the only one of us who has a phone in her room *and* her own personal phone number. This is great because it means we don't have to use a phone belonging to one of our parents — particularly while *they* might want to be using it. So we let Claud be VP, since we use her room and tie up her phone three times a week. Not to mention, eat her junk food.

The secretary of the club is Mary Anne, and boy is she good at it. I think she originally got the job because she has the tidiest handwriting of any of us. But she also turned out to be very organized, and thank goodness for that. Poor Mary Anne has the most complicated job of all. She's in charge of the club record book. That's where we keep track of all important information — our clients, their names and addresses, the money we earn, and *most* important, our sitting appointments. Mary Anne schedules everything on the appointment pages. In order to do this, she has to keep careful records, and also know, for instance, when Claud will be at an art class or Jessi at a ballet lesson or Mal at the orthodontist for her braces. Mary Anne has not made a single scheduling mistake.

Stacey is the treasurer, and she loves her job. For starters, she's a math whiz. She can empty out the money in our treasury (a manila envelope) and tell us how much is there practically just by looking at it. And she can add and subtract numbers in her head almost as fast as a computer could do it. (Well, I'm exaggerating a little, but she's a lot faster than any other club member.) Stacey's job is to collect club dues from us at every Monday meeting, to let us know if the treasury money is getting low, and to dole out money as we need it: to help pay Claud's monthly phone bill; to pay Charlie for driving Kristy to and from meetings, since she lives so far away now; to buy new things for the Kid-Kits; and to pay for an occasional sleepover or pizza party or something fun for the club! Stacey loves collecting money and hates parting with it. She keeps track of it in the record book and notes how we spend it.

I am the club's alternate officer, which is sort of like being a substitute teacher. It means I could take over the job of any other member who might have to miss a meeting. While Stacey was back in New York for that short time, I became the treasurer, but I was glad to give up the job when she returned. I'm not nearly as good at math as she is, and besides, everyone gets crabby when they have to pay their weekly dues. Even Kristy. I would much rather be the alternate officer. I get to do different jobs that way. I like the variety. But guess which job I've never been able to try — Kristy's. She has not missed *one* meeting. I'm dying to be president-for-a-day.

Jessi and Mal don't have actual jobs. "Junior Officer" means that they're allowed to baby-sit only after school and on weekend days. Their parents won't let them sit at night unless they're sitting for their own brothers and sisters. But believe me, two daytime-only club members are a big help. They free the rest of us up for nighttime jobs.

That's it for us BSC members. I guess the only other thing you need to know is that apart from the record book, Kristy makes us keep a club notebook. The notebook is more like a diary or journal. Each of us is responsible for writing up every single job we take, and then we're supposed to read the past week's entries to see what went on when our friends were sitting. Only Kristy and Mal actually like writing in the book, but we all admit that *reading* it is helpful. We see how our friends handled baby-sitting problems, and keep up with what's going on with the families we sit for regularly. It's always best to go to a job prepared — to know if a child is suddenly having nightmares or has developed a food allergy, anything like that.

Okay. So it was Monday and Claud's clock had hit five-thirty.

"Order!" called Kristy, relishing being in charge.

The rest of us sat up a little straighter. As usual, Jessi and Mal were on the floor. This time they were leaning against Claud's bed. They'd been putting sparkly stickers on their fingernails. Claud and Mary Anne and I were sitting in a row on Claudia's bed, and Stacey was sitting backwards in Claud's desk chair, resting her chin on the top rung. Sometimes I sit in the desk chair and Stacey sits on the bed. We trade off.

"Come to order," said Kristy again, just for good measure. *She* was sitting in Claud's director's chair, wearing a visor. A pencil was stuck over one ear, and the club notebook in her hand. "Okay, treasurer. Collect the dues."

Stacey gleefully got out the treasury envelope, while the rest of us groaned as we parted with our hard-earned money.

Then the phone began to ring and Mary Anne started lining up jobs for us. When we hit a lull, Claud said, "I'm hungry. Is anyone else?"

"I'm *starved*," replied Kristy.

Claudia found a bag of pretzels in her closet and passed them around. No one was surprised when Stacey didn't take any because her doctor has told her to be stricter than usual about between-meal snacks, even nonsugary ones. But we were sort of surprised when Mal passed them up.

"I don't feel too good," she confessed. She'd been quiet during the meeting.

"What's wrong?" asked Jessi, alarmed. And then, just like a mother, she put her hand to Mallory's forehead. "Hey, I think you've got a fever!" she exclaimed.

"Really?" said Mal weakly.

"Change places with me," Mary Anne spoke up. "You'll be more comfortable on the bed."

But Kristy said, "I think you should go home, Mal. You look terrible."

So Mal did go home. It was the first time any of us had left a meeting sick. We weren't worried, though. How sick could Mal be? She was able to ride her bicycle home.

CHAPTER 5

As it turned out, Mal was sicker than we'd guessed. By Wednesday she'd come down with . . . the chicken pox! Can you believe it? She's had the dreaded disease once before, but she'd caught it *again*, which is unusual.

"I bet she got it from Jamie and Lucy Newton," said Stacey at our Wednesday meeting. "*They* had it recently. And I think Mal sat for them just before their spots came out. They would have been contagious then."

"Well, we have a minor emergency on our hands," said Mary Anne. She had opened the record book and was studying the appointment pages. "Mal's got three jobs lined up during the next week or so. We better replace her on all of them. Who knows how long she'll be out of commission."

"When are the jobs?" asked Kristy.

Mary Anne told her. The second and third

jobs, it turned out, were easy to fill because only one other BSC member was available on each of those days. The first job presented a problem, though. It was at the Perkinses' house.

"Guess who's free that day," said Mary Anne in an odd voice.

"Who?" I asked.

"You and I."

"Oh." I knew my voice had sounded odd, too.

Usually when more than one of us is available to take a job, us BSC members are really nice about saying things like, "You go ahead and sit for Charlotte, Stacey. We know she's your favorite kid." Or, "You take it, Claud. You haven't had too many jobs lately."

But neither Mary Anne nor I said anything like that. We just looked at each other. Finally Mary Anne said, "I'd like the job."

"So would I," I replied honestly. Mary Anne didn't know it, but I was saving up to buy her a "now-we're-sisters" present. She had surprised me with one on the day of our parents' wedding, so now I wanted to get her one. I needed the extra money.

"But I," said Mary Anne, "am the one who had to move away from my old house. I used to live next door to the Perkinses and sit for them all the time. So I think I should get the job."

I glanced around the room. My friends looked surprised, as they always do when Mary Anne decides to stick up for herself. Kristy even looked a little pleased. She likes to see Mary Anne come out of her shell.

"Excuse me," I said, not sounding apologetic at all, "but I really *would* like that job. And I have just as much right to it as you have."

"Me, too." Mary Anne narrowed her eyes at me.

I narrowed mine back.

"You know," began Mary Anne, "I don't think my skirt looks so great on you, after all. It's a little . . . tight."

Everyone gasped.

"Are you implying that I'm fat?" I exclaimed, which was ridiculous, because I'm pretty thin.

"You said it, not me."

Our argument could have gone on quite awhile longer, but Kristy suddenly banged her fist down on Claudia's desk. The pencil cup rattled and we all jumped. Stacey jumped the highest, since she was sitting in the desk chair and got the brunt of the noise.

"Order!" cried Kristy. "This is extremely unprofessional, unbusinesslike behavior. As president, I won't stand for it. None of you other members should either. Now let's get this thing settled."

Kristy was practically roaring, but when the phone rang just then, she picked it up calmly and said sweetly, "Hello, Baby-sitters Club. How may we help you?"

The caller was Mrs. Newton, needing a sitter for Jamie and Lucy, and also wanting to apologize for Mal's catching the chicken pox again. "If I'd had *any* idea," she said to Kristy, "I'd never have asked Mallory to sit that day. But I didn't know that the kids had been exposed."

"Oh, *please* don't worry," said Kristy fervently. "These things happen when you're in our business. Besides, you're one of our best customers."

Kristy listened to Mrs. Newton for a few more moments. Then she said, "Okay, Mary Anne will check our schedule and I'll call you right back." She hung up. "The Newtons need a sitter for next Friday night until about eleven o'clock," she told Mary Anne. "Who's free?

And if it's you and Dawn, I don't even want to know about it."

Mary Anne glowered. "No," she said after she'd checked, "it's you and Stacey."

"You take it, Stace," said Kristy immediately. "You live much closer. It'll be easier. I'd have to ask Charlie or Mr. Newton to drive me."

"Thanks," replied Stacey casually.

Kristy turned to Dawn and me. "You see how easy that was?" she said, as if she'd just taken some medicine to prove that it could go down easily. Without waiting for an answer, she called Mrs. Newton to tell her who'd be sitting. Then she looked at my stepsister and me again. "All right," she said, "now which one of you is going to take the job with the Perkinses?"

"I am," said Mary Anne.

"I am," I said.

Kristy sighed. She looked at us as if we were two kindergartners fighting over something on the playground. "Okay, if you're going to act immature," she began, "we'll solve this the way Mom solves problems between David Michael and Karen. You two can draw straws."

I made a face, but what could I say? Mary Anne and I *were* being childish.

Besides, Kristy is the president.

Kristy took a piece of paper off of Claud's desk and tore it into two small strips. She made one longer than the other. Then she mixed them up and held them in one hand so that the tops were even.

"All right, Mary Anne, Dawn — each of you draw a straw. Whoever gets the longer one gets the job at the Perkinses'."

"Who draws first?" said Mary Anne immediately.

Kristy's patience was fading. "Dawn," she said testily. "You're drawing in alphabetical order according to first names."

I gloated at Mary Anne. Then I chose one of the pieces of paper.

Mary Anne took the other.

Hers was longer than mine.

"I got the job!" she cried. She gleefully made a change in the record book and then phoned Mrs. Perkins to let *her* know about the change.

I sat and stared at Claudia's bedspread. Was this fair? Was it? No, it was not. First Mary Anne caught my mother's bouquet at the wedding. Now she got the sitting job. Maybe sisters — excuse me, *step*sisters — were not all they were cracked up to be.

"Have fun at the job," I said sarcastically to

Mary Anne. "I hope the girls are monsters."

Mary Anne just smiled at me. The Perkins girls are never monsters.

Two nights later — Friday night — Mary Anne came home from the Perkinses'. It was about nine-thirty. I was lying on my bed, eating a granola bar and reading a book called *Ghosts: Fact and Fantasy.* I didn't even look up when Mary Anne entered our room.

"Hi," she said, after a few moments. She sat carefully on the edge of her bed.

"Hi," I replied. I still didn't look up.

"How's the book?"

"Fine."

"Well?"

"Well what?"

"Aren't you going to ask how the Perkinses are?"

Mary Anne had me there. If she'd said, "Aren't you going to ask how my job went?" I would have said, "No." But I like Myriah, Gabbie, and Laura — a lot. So I said, "Okay. How are the Perkinses?"

"Great, as usual. We really had fun."

"Good for you."

"Don't you want to know what the girls did?"

Well, of course I wanted to know: "What did they do?" I asked.

"All right. Laura slept most of the time." (Laura is just a baby.) "But Gabbie was rehearsing for a play she's going to be in at her preschool. It's called *The Three Piggy Opera*." (I couldn't help smiling.) "And guess what Myriah wanted to do?"

"What?" I asked. I admit it. I was hooked. I almost didn't care that Mary Anne had gotten the job and I hadn't.

"She wanted to write letters to famous people."

"You're kidding! . . . Can she write yet?" (Myriah is still in kindergarten.)

"Well, sort of. She can write her name, of course, and 'love' and a few other words. But she needed a lot of help. She wanted to write to the president to tell him she'd lost a tooth. And then she wanted to write to — get this — *Cam Geary* to tell him he's her favorite star."

Mary Anne and I were both laughing by then. See, the funny thing is, Cam Geary is *Mary Anne's* favorite star. I had put my book down, sat up, and was facing Mary Anne on her bed.

"What did the letters say?" I asked.

Mary Anne smiled. "The first one went:

'Dear Mr. President, I have lost a tooth. It was a bottom tooth. I put it under my pillow and the Tooth Fairy came. She left me a prize. I just thought you would want to know. Love, Myriah. P.S. Keep up the good work.' "

"Oh, that is so *cute!*" I exclaimed. "Myriah is such a great kid."

"So's Gabbie," replied Mary Anne. "You should have heard her singing. She was rehearsing really hard."

"How about the letter to Cam Geary?" I asked.

"Oh, that one went: 'Dear Cam, Hi! How are you? My name is Myriah and I am your favorite fan.' "

"Your *favorite* fan?" I repeated.

"I think she meant 'biggest.' Anyway, then she went on: 'I like your TV show very much. If you're ever in Stoneybrook, come visit me. I live on Bradford Court. I'd be happy to give you some cookies. Love, Myriah.' "

Well, leave it to the Perkins girls. Mary Anne and I were friends again. No, I think we were sisters again. How could we help it, after sharing a story like that one?

When we went to sleep that night we both said, " 'Night, sis."

CHAPTER 6

Satruday

Yisterday I sat at the Piks house boy was mal a pain. Sory you' will read this wehn your beter mal but you were a pain. maybe you didn't lick being babbysat for agian, but I couldn't' help it. Your mother called becuase she needed to take the ~~Dr~~ ~~Dr~~ triplits to the doctor so that left you and Niky and yoire sisters. I hope you feel beter soon realy I do. Realy.

I guess if I were eleven, a baby-sitter myself, and not feeling well, I wouldn't have been a terrific sitting charge, either, so maybe it's understandable that Mallory did not give Claudia an easy time that afternoon. (Claud told us about her experience later that day at our meeting.)

For one thing, Mal was in an odd position. She was half baby-sitter (even though she was confined to her bedroom) and half baby-sittee. Mrs. Pike needed a sitter desperately (I'll tell you why in a minute), but even though Claud had already had the chicken pox, Mrs. Pike didn't want her going too close to Mal because now we knew that it was possible to get the pox again. Therefore, Claud had to take care of Mal as best she could without going in her room. However, with so many other Pike kids around, Mal was considered an extra baby-sitter, just in case of an emergency.

Anyway, Adam, Byron, and Jordan (the triplets) had not been feeling well lately. They'd been coughing, sounded congested in their chests, and had been very tired. So Mrs. Pike decided a trip to the doctor was in order. Claud was left in charge of Vanessa, Nicky, Margo, Claire, and the itchy, crabby Mallory.

(By the way, Claire is five, Margo is seven, Nicky is eight, and Vanessa is nine.)

"Let's play doctor's office!" said Claire as soon as Mrs. Pike and the triplets had left. With so much sickness in her house, no wonder she wanted to do that. "Okay," agreed Margo instantly.

But Nicky and Vanessa were harder to convince. In the end, Claud said, she thinks they only gave in because it was raining, and anyway, if they'd said no, their little sisters would just have begged them nonstop.

"Oh, goody!" sang Claire when everyone had agreed to play. "Now look, you silly-billy-goo-goos. The whole rec room is the doctor's office. No, wait. It's the emergency room. No, a hospital. A hospital, okay? Oh, and here comes the ambulance. Right now! There's an emergency!"

Claudia could see the others getting into the spirit of the game.

"Ooh-eee-ooh," wailed Nicky helpfully.

"Make way for the ambulance!" cried Claire.

"I'll be the special emergency-room doctor," said Vanessa. "Hey, wait a sec. We need props." She dug around in a bin of toys and came up with a stethoscope for herself, plus a nurse's cap, a rolled-up bandage, a gigantic

51

fake syringe, and a doctor's kit. She handed the nurse's cap to Nicky.

"Here, you be the nurse," she said. "I'm the doctor."

"No way!" exclaimed Nicky. "Doctors are boys and nurses are girls."

"Oh, that is so old-fashioned," said Vanessa. "There are lots of women doctors today. You know that very well. Doctor Dellenkamp is a woman."

"Well, I am *not* going to be a boy nurse," replied Nicky. He handed the cap to Margo. "I'm going to be the ambulance driver."

"And I'll be the patient," said Claire. "I was just in a very, very terrible car accident. I am all bloody and I think my leg is broken. My head, too."

(Claudia succeeded in not laughing.)

"Okay. I'll get you to the hospital in a jiffy," said Nicky. He slid Claire across the floor. "Ambulance coming!" he yelled.

Vanessa and Margo ran to their patient.

"Check her blood pressure," Vanessa instructed the nurse. Then she added, just like on the TV shows, "I can't find a pulse!"

"It's in her wrist, dummy," hissed Margo.

Claire continued to lie on the floor. Her eyes looked closed, but Claud could tell she was peeking, trying to watch what was going on.

"What happened to the victim?" Vanessa asked Nicky.

"Car accident, ma'am. She was riding her bike and she ran into a truck."

"I did not!" Claire whispered loudly. "The truck ran into me."

Vanessa was giving Claire an injection with the toy syringe when Claud first heard Mallory's bell ringing upstairs.

Ding, ding, ding!

"Oh," said Claud, "Mal's calling. I better go see what she wants."

Claudia dashed up to Mallory and Vanessa's room. The door was open, but only a crack.

"Mal?" called Claud.

"Claudia?" Mal replied. "Don't come in. Mom said for you to stay away from me. Just in case."

"I know. Do you need something?"

"A soda," Mal replied grumpily. "I'm thirsty. And bored."

"Sorry," Claud told her honestly. "I'll have Vanessa bring you a drink, but I can't come in and talk to you or anything. Don't you have a book to read?"

"I read two today."

"How about writing in your journal?"

"I've written ten pages."

"Is the portable TV in there?"

"Yes, but there's nothing on except reruns and boring talk shows."

Claud sighed. She was out of suggestions. "I'll have Vanessa get your drink. What do you want?"

"Ginger ale," said Mal in a tiny, pathetic voice.

So Claud interrupted the hospital game to ask Vanessa to take the ginger ale to her sick sister. While Vanessa was gone, Margo, still wearing the nurse's cap, said, "Okay, now I'm a mother and Claire is my little boy — "

"*Boy?*" cried Claire.

"Yes, *boy*. And he's just fallen down the stairs."

Claire immediately crumpled to the floor.

"And I'm the doctor," said Nicky, grabbing for the stethoscope, which Vanessa had left on the floor.

"Oh! Oh, doctor!" cried Margo immediately. She tried to pick Claire up, but she wasn't strong enough, so she dragged her over to Nicky by the legs. "My little boy fell down the stairs! Oh, no! Help! What am I going to do?"

Before Nicky could answer, Vanessa made an announcement from the head of the stairs.

"Mallory is itchy," she said. "She wants to take a baking-soda bath."

"I'll go talk to her," said Claudia, and she ran up the stairs again. "Mal?" she called through the crack in the door. She thought it was awfully frustrating not to be able to *see* Mallory.

"Can I take a baking-soda bath?" asked Mal. "It helped a lot last night. You can't believe how much I itch. I feel like I have poison ivy."

"I'm sorry," said Claudia. "That must be awful. I remember when I — "

"Can I *please* take a bath?" Mal interrupted her.

"I think you should wait until your mom gets home."

"I *knew* you were going to say that."

If she knew it, Claud thought, then why did she ask? But she reminded herself that Mallory felt really lousy. "Why don't you play with your Kid-Kit?" she teased.

At last she got a laugh out of Mal. "Maybe I'll read some more after all," she said.

"Or how about a nap?" suggested Claud. "I'm serious. You might feel better."

"Okay."

Claud returned to the game in the rec room. Nicky was now the patient. He had fallen off a building in New York City and had broken every bone in his body. "Doctor, doctor," he mumbled, "will I ever play the violin again?"

"I think so," replied Dr. Vanessa. "Yes, I think so."

"That's funny," said Nicky. "I could never play before!" He convulsed in laughter.

"Patient," said Vanessa, "you cut that out. You can't do that with broken bones."

Nicky couldn't stop laughing at his joke. The three girls looked at each other helplessly.

Finally Claire said, "I'll be the doctor now."

"No, you won't. I'm the doctor!" cried Vanessa.

"It's my turn!"

"No way!"

"I'm telling Mallory!"

"No, you're not," Claudia broke in. "Mallory's trying to take a nap."

"I am not," called Mallory from upstairs. "I can't sleep. I'm thirsty again."

So Vanessa brought Mal some more ginger ale. Claire was just about to come down with appendicitis when the back door opened and in walked Mrs. Pike, followed by the very pale triplets.

"Mommy!" Claire cried. "I have appendicitis and Nicky fell off a skyscraper."

56

"Oh, I hope not," said Mrs. Pike, and she looked so distressed that Claudia asked worriedly, "What's wrong?"

"The doctor thinks the boys have pneumonia," replied Mrs. Pike.

"*All* of them?" asked Claudia. "I didn't know it was catching."

"Usually it isn't, but they've got some viral form. They'll have to be kept isolated in their bedroom. Claudia, don't you get too close to them."

"No," said Claudia, backing away.

"Oh, dear. How am I going to keep them quiet until they're well?"

"Don't worry, Mom," spoke up Jordan, who had sunk into a chair. "I don't think I can move." But he did. He managed to follow his brothers upstairs.

"Four sick kids," moaned Mrs. Pike. "I guess I should be used to it. Once, all eight of them had a stomach virus at the same time."

"Ew," said Claudia. And then she remembered poor Mal. "Oh, by the way," she added. "Mallory is dying to take another baking-soda bath. She really itches."

· "Okay." Mrs. Pike nodded wearily.

"Can I stay and help you with anything?" asked Claudia.

"Oh, that would be wonderful," replied Mrs. Pike, looking relieved.

"I can stay until five-fifteen," said Claud. "Then I'll have to leave for our BSC meeting."

"Great. Can you watch Vanessa, Margo, Claire, and Nicky while I go take care of the others? I'll get the triplets settled and help Mallory with her bath."

No sooner had Mrs. Pike dashed upstairs than Claire began talking again. "Now this time," she said, "Margo has been caught in a hurricane. And a tornado. And Vanessa is her mother, who's looking for her. I'm the doctor, waiting at the hospital. . . ."

The game was still going on when Claudia left.

CHAPTER 7

I used to like weekends better than week-days — for the obvious reasons. I could sleep late, I didn't have to go to school, I had free time, I could go shopping. Ever since the wedding, though, I've liked the weekdays better. You want to know why? I'll tell you why. Because on the weekends everyone is around all the time (well, usually), and Richard and Mary Anne are driving me crazy.

I have never seen anyone as neat as Richard. And he's not just neat, he has these systems for everything. For instance, he has organized all our books into categories, such as fiction, nonfiction, poetry, plays, and reference. And within each category, the books are arranged alphabetically according to the author's last name. And Richard's clothes are arranged not only by type but by color. In his closet hang (from left to right) his white shirts, his yellow shirts, then his blue shirts, from lighter to darker.

And little changes have crept into our house. For the first time ever, there are dividers in the kitchen drawers, so we have a place for the spoons, a place for the forks, etc. Even our refrigerator is organized. Richard put all these special holders in it so that we have certain spots for eggs, for cans of seltzer, you name it.

Now, I happen to like being organized (within reason), but my mother is an incurable slob, which can cause problems. I am now going to describe a typical Saturday at my house:

Richard wakes up around six o'clock. He gets up early no matter what day it is. He starts brewing coffee in his coffee-maker. While the coffee's going, he gets the newspaper. He reads it in this order: business news, international news, national news, and local news. He sets the rest of the paper aside.

He does his reading while he drinks his coffee. He always makes exactly one and a half cups. That's the perfect amount for him. No one else in the house drinks coffee. Then he washes out the coffeepot, puts his mug in the dishwasher, and starts breakfast.

The rest of us come downstairs all bleary-eyed anywhere from eight o'clock until ten o'clock. Mom always sleeps the latest and Richard always says to her, "I'd just about given up on you. I hope your breakfast still tastes okay."

If he knows she's going to get up so late, why does he start cooking so early?

But Mom just kisses him and tells him that she's sure breakfast will be okay, and that anything he's cooked is fine with her. (Which isn't true, because she never eats the bacon, and she doesn't like waffles or pancakes.)

After breakfast, Mom strews the newspaper all over the living room while she reads it, and Richard tidies it up and puts the sections back together — in order. (What's the point? We're just going to get rid of it.) Then Mom goes upstairs and showers and dresses. She leaves her nightgown on the floor and wet towels all over the bathroom. Richard comes along and picks everything up.

At this point, Mom sometimes gets mad. "I can clean up after myself!" she protests.

"But you never do," replies Richard.

Once Mom is dressed, we either do something together as a family or go our separate ways. Mom likes movies, shopping, or going to a park for a picnic. Richard likes driving to Stamford and visiting museums, taking in a matinee (of a play, not a movie), or going out for a fancy meal. I like going our separate ways. I would much rather baby-sit than go to an art museum.

Then comes dinner. If we don't eat out, then Mom cooks. She is trying to convert Richard and Mary Anne to our vegetarian, health-food way of eating. She is not having much luck.

Mary Anne tries to kid about it. She says, "Where's the beef?"

Richard is more direct. He comes right out and says, "Can't we have a little meat *some*-times? Mary Anne and I are used to it."

"Have it at lunch during the week," was Mom's answer once. "Then I won't have to look at it."

In all honesty, I think Mom can go a little overboard. That was a rude comment. She didn't have to talk to Richard like that.

So anyway, with Mom cooking, we end up eating our usual brown rice and vegetables, or tofu salad or something. After dinner, Mom wanders off to watch TV unless she and Richard are going out. Richard waits until he can't stand it any longer. Then he makes Mary Anne and me help him clean up the kitchen.

This really is not fair. Not that Mary Anne and I have to help him, but that he has to clean up the kitchen *again* (because, of course, he cleaned it up after breakfast).

The problem here is not that Mom would *never* clean up the kitchen, but that she might not get to it until the next day. She's just loose about those things and Richard is rigid about them.

I can't imagine why I didn't see these problems *before* they got married.

One Saturday — the Saturday after the Pike Plague had started — our usual day began. I dragged my eyes open at nine o'clock. Mary Anne's bed was empty. (One part of it was full of cat fur. Tigger sleeps with her every night in the same spot, and he sheds.)

I lay in my bed and enjoyed the peace and quiet. I could tell that the weather was nice because I could see sunshine peeking around the window shades. The day stretched ahead of me. I didn't have a thing to do. I mean — nothing I'd planned to do. My homework was finished and I didn't have a baby-sitting job. I rolled out of bed, took my time in the bathroom, and then padded barefoot into the kitchen.

There were Mary Anne and her dad seated at the table, eating breakfast. In a corner by the refrigerator, Tigger was eating *his* breakfast. (It smelled awful.)

"Morning," I said, feeling like a stranger in my own kitchen, even though both Richard and Mary Anne smiled at me, and Richard served me breakfast right away.

"Guess what we've decided today is going to be," said Richard, smiling.

Uh-oh. What?

"What?" I asked.

"Spring-cleaning day!" announced Mary Anne.

I just looked at them. Finally I said, "In my whole life, I have never spring cleaned."

"Well, there's no time like the present to start," said Richard. He is always coming out with sayings like that.

Wait'll Mom hears about this, I thought, but all I said was, "I think Mom wanted to go to Washington Mall today."

"Oh, well. She can go tomorrow," said Richard. "The stores are open on Sunday."

I almost said that there was no time like the present, but I didn't.

When Mom finally came downstairs, Richard kissed her gently (I like it when they look so much in love, even though it's embarrassing), and then he said (what else?), "I'd just about given up on you. I hope your breakfast still tastes okay."

I don't now whether it did or not, but Mom ate everything except the bacon. She never eats it and Richard always serves it to her.

Then Richard broke the news to Mom about spring cleaning. She took it well, since she is so laid-back.

The cleaning began. I could tell that Mom's mind was a million miles away. She just sort of drifted through the house with a dust rag, wiping stuff from tables onto the floor.

Mary Anne followed her around with the Dustbuster.

"That is so rude," I told her.

"Well, your mother isn't cleaning. She's just moving the mess to the floor. She's brushed flower petals, cat fur, and kitty litter onto the floor and left it there."

"She doesn't realize what she's doing," I replied. "And furthermore, the cat fur and kitty litter wouldn't be there if Tigger weren't."

"No, the kitty litter wouldn't be there if *Dad and I* weren't. Tigger went to the bathroom outside at our old house. But he's afraid to go outside here. So he uses the litter box."

"Hmphh."

Just to get back at Mary Anne, I tiptoed upstairs to our parents' bedroom. I opened the sock drawer in Richard's bureau. There were neatly matched rows of socks — in alphabetical order by color. I switched a pair of brown socks with a pair of gray ones.

I knew it would drive Richard crazy.

Then I glanced around the bedroom. It looked like it was being shared by Felix Unger and Oscar Madison, the Odd Couple. So I straightened up Mom's messy half of the room. On Richard's neat half, I "accidentally" dropped a tissue.

By six o'clock that night, the house was spic-and-span. The tissue was even gone from the bedroom floor. However, Richard had discovered that his socks were out of order. It *had* driven him crazy because he thought it was his fault. So as you can imagine, what with Mary Anne and the Dustbuster and Richard and his socks, no one was in a very good mood, despite the clean house.

Except for Mom. Ever cheerful, she said, "Let's order in Chinese food. Then those of you who want meat can have it, and the rest of us can eat vegetarian."

So that was exactly what we did. And we actually had a nice dinner. We ate on trays in front of the TV. We even agreed on a movie to watch on the VCR. The trouble arose when we had finished eating. Mom wanted to watch the rest of the movie and then clean up. (I think Mary Anne did, too.) But Richard wanted to stop the movie, clean up, and then watch the rest of the movie. Personally, I thought that was a good idea, because it's best to get leftover food in the fridge as soon as possible, but I felt I had to stick up for Mom.

"The dishes can wait, can't they?" I asked.

After a pause, Mary Anne said, "I think we should clean up."

"Then clean up," I snapped.

(Mom was oblivious to this. She was engrossed in the movie.)

So Richard and Mary Anne cleaned up the kitchen while Mom and I watched TV. About a half an hour later, Mary Anne stuck her head in the room and announced, "*I'm* going over to *Kristy's*. Thanks for a *lovely* day, Dawn. You won't have to see me again until tomorrow because I'm spending the ni — "

She was interrupted by a gagging sound. It even attracted Mom's attention.

Tigger was throwing up on our Oriental rug.

"Oh, no!" cried Mary Anne. She rushed Tigger into the kitchen in case he got sick again. Then she returned with some paper towels to clean up the mess. She found my mother in a pretty bad mood.

"Look what your cat did!"

Even I hadn't expected Mom the slob to say that. She'd never cared about our rugs before.

Mary Anne was so nervous about Tigger and my mother that she stayed home after all. I couldn't blame her.

What a day, what a day.

CHAPTER 8

Almost a week later — on Friday night — Mary Anne and I were still arguing about everything, and Mallory and the triplets were still sick. The doctor had said that Mal had a worse case of the pox than before since she was older. And the triplets were just plain in bad shape.

Anyway, we were holding yet another meeting without Mallory, and scrambling around, trying to fill all the job offers that came in. We'd had to call on both Logan and Shannon for help. As the meeting came to a close and the phone stopped ringing, Stacey said, "So what's everyone wearing tonight?"

"For what?" I asked.

"For the *dance*," said Mary Anne.

Oh, yeah. I'd forgotten about it. Everyone in the club, except for Jessi and me, was going. Jessi wasn't going because the dance was only for eighth-graders, and I wasn't going because I hadn't been invited.

"I'm wearing my pink dress," said Claudia. "The short one. And my earrings that look like globes. Oh, and a necklace I made from candy."

"You had candy in your room and you didn't *eat* it?" I said.

Everyone laughed. And Claud's clock turned to six.

Good. Time to go. We could get off the subject of the dance. I hated the fact that no boy had asked me to go. (But I had to admit that I was looking forward to an evening at home without Mary Anne.)

That night, as soon as dinner was over, Mary Anne ran upstairs. "Help me find something to wear!" she called over her shoulder.

Oh, yuck. That was like rubbing salt in a wound. I felt bad enough that I hadn't been invited to the dance. But if helping Mary Anne would speed things along and get her out of the house faster, then I would do it.

I followed her to our room.

"I am *so* glad to be going to this dance," said Mary Anne.

Was she gloating — or just glad to leave the

house for awhile? If I were Mary Anne, I wouldn't have minded leaving. I was certainly looking forward to my evening alone. (Well, Mom and Richard would be home, but I planned to stay upstairs and just read and veg out and enjoy the peace.)

"You're lucky to be going, especially with Logan," I said.

Mary Anne smiled. "Yeah. And I want to look my best for him. Now let's see. The last time we went to a dance I wore my green jumpsuit. . . . Hey, could I borrow that really short, flared skirt of yours? The blue one with the black waistband? I could wear my baggy white shirt with it."

Anything, anything.

Mary Anne got dressed. She looked at herself in the mirror for ages. "When you have a boyfriend," she told me, "you want to look good for him."

"Maybe *you* do," I said, "but *I* would rather find a guy I could be a slob around."

"You probably picked that up from your mom," said Mary Anne.

I really don't think she intended that as an insult. She said it while she was frantically taking stuff out of one purse and putting it in another. She was just trying to make conversation and she couldn't wait to get out of the house — I think.

I didn't blame her. The house didn't feel like *ours* yet. It still seemed like Mom's and mine. Mary Anne and her dad and Tigger just happened to live in it, too. Mary Anne must have felt like a guest in a hotel. So I tried to forgive her for the comments and for bragging about Logan.

I did not think, though, that it was necessary for her to call, as she and her father were heading out the door, "Just try to enjoy the evening, Dawn. Don't think of yourself as someone who can't get a date, okay? It isn't healthy."

Well, that did it. I marched upstairs to the phone in Mom's and Richard's room and called Jeff in California. It was eight o'clock here, which meant it was five o'clock there. Jeff *might* be home.

Ring . . . ring . . . ri —

Someone picked up the phone. An unfamiliar woman's voice said, "Hello, Schafer residence."

I knew it wasn't Dad's housekeeper.

"Is — is Jeff there?" I asked. Maybe I'd dialed the wrong number.

"Hold on a sec," said the woman.

A few moments later I heard Jeff say, "Hello?"

"Hi, Jeff!" I replied excitedly. "It's me, Dawn."

"Hi!" Jeff sounded as excited as I felt. It's funny, but we've grown closer since he moved back to California.

"Who answered the phone just now?" I asked. "Did Dad get a new housekeeper?"

"Just a sec," said Jeff. There was a long pause. At last he said in a soft, muffled voice. "That was Carol, Dad's new girlfriend. I had to wait for her to leave the room."

"What's she doing over there?" I wanted to know.

"She's going to have dinner with us. She's here a lot."

"Do you like her?"

I just knew that at the other end of the three thousand miles of telephone wires my brother was shrugging. "She's okay, I guess."

"Do you think Dad really likes her?"

"Yeah . . . I do. But I don't think they're going to get married or anything."

"How come?"

"Because Carol keeps saying, 'I'll never marry anyone.' " (Jeff was speaking in a high, squeaky voice, and I giggled.) "She says, 'The last thing I want is to have the responsibility of a family.' But you'd never know that from all the time she spends with Dad and me. Anyway, how are you? How are things going with Mary Anne and her father?"

"You mean Mary Anne and 'sir'?"

Jeff laughed. "I couldn't help that. He's so stiff and formal."

"Tidy, too," I added. I told my brother about the sock drawer, and Jeff laughed again. "You know what I like about you?" I said.

"My good looks?" replied Jeff.

"Apart from your looks."

"What?"

"You're dependable. And predictable. I used to think Mary Anne was, too, but now I'm not so sure." And then something dawned on me. "That must be because you're my *real* brother but Mary Anne is only my *step*sister." I told Jeff about some of the things Mary Anne had said and done recently. "I never would have expected her to brag about Logan the way she did tonight," I finished up.

"You know what?" said Jeff. "That reminded me of something. I've never talked about this with anyone, but I know it's true: when *she's* around — " (I knew Jeff meant Carol) " — I act different than when she isn't.

Like, when she's over at the house, sometimes I feel I'm being squeezed."

"Squeezed?"

"It's hard to explain. I just can't always be myself around her. And she takes up space. I mean, she doesn't really take up much, of course. 'Cause she's not fat." (I smiled.) "It's more like . . ."

"Emotional space?" I supplied. I was thinking of the Arnold girls, Marilyn and Carolyn, whom the club sits for sometimes. They're identical twins, but they're two very different people, with different interests, different taste, and different friends. And recently they hadn't been getting along. It turned out that they needed separate bedrooms to go with their separate lives. They needed emotional space in order to be friends. At least, that was how I thought of the problem.

"Emotional space?" Jeff repeated. "Yeah, I guess that describes it."

My *real* brother and I talked awhile longer, but finally we had to get off the phone. Mom is nice about letting us call each other and I didn't want to take advantage of that. Besides, I'd noticed that Richard scrutinized our phone bill. I mean *every little detail*.

After Jeff and I hung up I wandered into my

room. I read for awhile. Then I decided to go to bed early, so I called good night to Mom and Richard, turned off my light, and fell into a deep sleep.

I'm not sure how much later it happened, but the next thing I knew, I was awake — unhappily. The light was on in our room and Mary Anne was moving around, putting on her nightgown and calling, "Tigger! Tigger?" If she was trying to whisper, she wasn't doing a very good job.

"Mrrumphh," I said, rolling onto my stomach and putting the pillow over my head.

"Oh, Dawn. Sorry. Did I wake you?" asked Mary Anne.

"No, no. I was going to get up anyway. It's time for my next feeding."

Mary Anne giggled.

I peeked out from under the pillow. "Can you turn the light off? It's killing my eyes."

"Sure." Mary Anne hit the light, then fumbled over to her bed. "Dawn?" she said. "The dance was fun. Everyone missed you."

"Really?"

"Of course. You should have come anyway. Logan would have danced with you. Besides, half the kids there arrived without dates. It didn't matter."

I was beginning to feel better. Also, more awake. "So what went on?" I asked. "Did anything happen?"

"Let's see. Alan Gray was doing that thing where he puts M&Ms in his eyes, and he did it so often that Kristy got mad at him and they had a fight."

"I thought Kristy invited Bart Taylor to the dance," I said.

"She did. Alan just wanted to drive her crazy by hanging around her and looking like Little Orphan Annie. He succeeded, too."

Mary Anne told me about the rest of the dance then — who had had fun, who hadn't, what everyone had worn.

I began to think of her as my sister again, instead of my *step*sister. I was very confused. How could we get along so well half the time and be mad at each other the rest of the time? Was this what having a sister was all about?

CHAPTER 9

Saturday

The Pike Plague continues. The things that can happen to a family are just amazing. I guess when you have eight kids you sort of learn to expect the unexpected. But I'm an only child. I'm also a pretty careful person. I haven't broken any bones or had too many accidents in my life. I'm sick a lot, but that's not my fault. Anyway, I'm off the subject.

I arrived at the Pikes' this afternoon to find that Nicky had re-broken that finger he once broke, plus broken two others playing some game in gym yesterday, so he wasn't in such hot shape. Then, while I was baby-sitting, Vanessa had an accident....

The most unusual thing about Vanessa's accident, Stacey pointed out, was that she had one at all. Vanessa is the Pike poet (or maybe I should say poetess). She is not an athletic person. Her favorite activity is sitting somewhere (in private, if possible, which is difficult at her house), and writing her poetry. She's got volumes of it.

But on the day that Stacey sat for the Pikes, Vanessa decided she needed some exercise.

"I want to keep my strength up," she told Stacey, "so that I don't catch the triplets' pneumonia or Mallory's chicken pox."

"I don't blame you," replied Stacey.

I might add here that Stacey was wearing a surgeon's mask that afternoon. It wasn't her idea (it was Mrs. Pike's and her mother's), but Stacey had gone along with it willingly. *She* didn't want to catch pneumonia or get the pox back, either, and she'd been assured that she wouldn't if she wore the mask, at least while she was indoors. Also, the weather was beautiful, and Mrs. Pike had told Stacey that she could watch Vanessa, Margo, and Claire outside for part of the time, as long as she left the back door open so she could hear Mal, the triplets, or Nicky if they needed anything.

Stacey had earmarked this particular job as an easy one, with five of the eight Pikes laid up.

Boy, was she wrong.

Mr. and Mrs. Pike needed a sitter because they had had tickets for ages to some tennis match in Stamford. The tickets were expensive and the Pikes didn't want to miss the game; otherwise they might have stayed at home with their ailing family. But they are tennis nuts, so off they went.

As soon as they had left, Stacey, her mask in place, stood at the bottom of the steps and yelled upstairs, "Anybody need anything?"

"Ginger ale," replied Mal.

"Water," replied Byron.

"A Popsicle," replied Adam.

"More Kleenex," replied Jordan.

"My dinosaurs," replied a fifth voice. That was Nicky on the couch in the living room. He sounded bored to death.

Stacey sighed. Then she got to work. When she had assembled the ginger ale, water, Popsicle, and Kleenex on a tray, she sent the things upstairs with Vanessa, who returned with Nicky's dinosaurs and handed them to him.

Possibly sensing that she might become an

errand girl for the afternoon, it was at this point that Vanessa said something about needing exercise and then added, "I think I'll go outside and ride my bike, okay, Stacey?"

"Okay," Stacey answered. "Be careful. And if you're going to leave the neighborhood, let me know." (A good baby-sitter keeps careful track of her charges at all times.)

"I will." Vanessa left quickly.

"Claire? Margo?" Stacey called then, realizing that she hadn't seen them since she'd arrived about fifteen minutes earlier.

"Down here!" called Margo from the rec room. "We're playing hospital."

Again? thought Stacey, as she went downstairs.

"Hi, Stacey-silly-billy-goo-goo!" cried Claire. "You know what? This game isn't easy with only two people. I have to be the ambulance driver, the doctor, *and* the X-ray person."

"And I'm the patient, the nurse, and the worried mother," added Margo.

"You're the patient *and* a nurse?" said Stacey, smiling. "That *must* be tough."

"It is. But someone's got to do it."

"Now, Margo," said Claire, who usually directed these games, "there's a terrible fire, okay? And you got caught in it. In your car. And your car blew up.''

Gosh, thought Stacey. Playing hospital sure had changed. When she was little, all she and her friends ever did when they played hospital was catch colds or fall down. Maybe once in awhile one of them would get appendicitis. But that was the worst that would happen.

Stacey let Claire and Margo play a little longer. Then she said, ''Don't you want to go outside, you guys? It's such a nice day. If you played outside you could use the wagon for an ambulance.'' (And I could take off this stupid mask, she thought.)

The girls thought that over. At last Claire said, ''Let's go!''

''Great,'' said Stacey. ''Let me just see if anyone upstairs needs anything. Then I'll be right out. You go ahead.''

Claire and Margo ran out the back door and Stacey called up to the ailing Pikes, ''Anyone need anything?''

She braced herself for the replies. But all she got was a chorus of ''No, thanks!'' Surprised, she went outside.

For awhile, Stacey just sat on the patio and watched the game of hospital continue. She took off the surgeon's mask. The girls battled a flood, a tornado, and a plane crash. Each time, the wonderful doctor at the hospital saved the terribly sick or wounded patient.

Claire was in the middle of saving Margo's life yet again when Vanessa came hurtling up the driveway on her bicycle. She was riding too fast and Stacey knew it. For that reason, Stacey was already on her feet when Vanessa tried to put on her brakes at the end of the driveway and skidded into a nearby cherry tree instead.

"Ow, ow, ow!" she cried.

Stacey reached her in two seconds. "Oh, Vanessa," she said. "Wow. What a fall. Okay, don't move too fast. Did you hit your head?"

Vanessa sat up slowly. "No," she said, shaking it, "but my elbow hurts. So does my ankle."

"Doctor Claire to the rescue!" cried Claire, as she and Margo raced to the scene of the accident.

"Hold on, Claire," said Stacey gently. "This is a real accident. I need to take a good look at our patient. Okay, I see which elbow you hurt, Vanessa. It's pretty scraped up."

"I think I scraped it on that gravel," she said, pointing.

Stacey examined the wound. "There's still

some gravel in it," she announced. "Now, which ankle hurts?"

"My left one," replied Vanessa.

"It *looks* okay," said Stacey. "Try to stand on it."

Vanessa struggled to her feet, but immediately fell down again, clutching her ankle. "That *hurts!*" she exclaimed, gasping.

"Okay," said Stacey calmly. "I think you better see your doctor."

"Goody!" cried Claire. "Well, here I am."

"No, I mean the real one," said Stacey. "Margo, can you help make your sister comfortable? I've got to make a few phone calls."

Stacey dashed inside. She called Claudia, who wasn't at home. Next she tried me. "Hi, Dawn? Oh, thank goodness you're there. Can you come over to the Pikes' right away? Vanessa had an accident. . . . Great." Then Stacey hung up and called her mother. "Can you drive us to the doctor's office?" she asked when she explained what had happened.

"Of course," replied her mother immediately.

Mrs. McGill and I arrived at the Pikes' at the same time. Stacey, her mom, and I loaded Vanessa into the back of the McGills' station wagon. Then I stood in the driveway with

Claire and Margo, and the three of us watched as the car backed down the driveway.

"There goes the ambulance," murmured Margo.

And Claire added, "Ooh-eee-ooh. . . . See you later, Vanessa-silly-billy-goo-goo."

Meanwhile, Stacey's mother sped toward the doctor's office.

"Faster! Faster!" Stacey kept crying.

"Honey," her mother replied, "this isn't an emergency, luckily. And I don't want to get a speeding ticket."

"I'm okay," spoke up Vanessa. "Gosh, I wonder which doctor I'll see. There are three of them in the group, but only one is around on Saturdays."

The doctor on duty was Dr. Dellenkamp, whom Vanessa likes a lot. Even when she had to work a little to get the gravel out of Vanessa's wound, and when she sprayed it with antiseptic, and again when she wrapped an ace bandage around Vanessa's sprained ankle, Vanessa just said, "Ow!"

Stacey stayed with her the whole time while her mother sat in the waiting room. "I *should* stay with her, Mom," Stacey had told Mrs. McGill. "I'm the baby-sitter."

* * *

Stacey, her mother, and Vanessa returned to the Pikes' about fifteen minutes before Mr. and Mrs. Pike got back. There was just enough time for me to leave and for Stacey to settle Vanessa on the other couch in the living room with Nicky.

"Thanks, Dawn!" Stacey called as I left. "I owe you one."

"No problem!" I called back.

When the Pikes pulled into their driveway, Claire greeted them. "Guess what," she said before they'd even gotten out of their car. "Vanessa fell off her bike and Stacey took her to the hospital in an ambulance and Vanessa's *ankle* is *broken!*"

No wonder the Pikes were in a panic when they dashed into the living room. They ran to Vanessa, where they saw an ordinary ace bandage, not a cast, on her ankle. Vanessa was drinking a ginger ale and looking pretty jolly.

"I sprained it," she said, almost proudly. "I can't even walk on it. I got crutches, see?" Vanessa pointed to the crutches, which Stacey had propped up against one end of the couch.

"I see," said Mrs. Pike wearily, "but I don't believe it. Six ailing children. What's going to happen next?"

"Nothing," said Mr. Pike firmly. "Absolutely nothing."

"Doctor Dellenkamp said you could call her if you have any questions," Stacey told the Pikes, who had thanked her several times for her quick thinking and for handling a tough situation so well.

"Okay," they replied. "We'll phone the doctor right away."

Then Mr. Pike called upstairs, "How's everybody doing? Does anyone need anything?"

"Something new to read, Dad," said Mal.

"Cookies," said Jordan.

"Grapes," said Adam.

"A sandwich," said Byron.

"My sanity," said Mrs. Pike.

CHAPTER 10

Monday. Five-thirty. My friends and I were gathering for another meeting of the Baby-sitters Club. We started arriving around five-fifteen.

Surprisingly, I had been the first to reach BSC headquarters. I was even there before Claudia. She had a sitting job with Jamie and Lucy Newton. It was running a little overtime. In the old days, if I had arrived and Claudia hadn't been there, I probably would have chatted with Mimi, Claudia's grandmother. I had liked our chats. But Mimi was gone now.

Janine, Claudia's sister, told me to wait in Claud's bedroom, so I did, thumbing through the notebook to see what had happened in the last week. I wondered what Mary Anne and Kristy were up to. They'd gone to Kristy's house after school, something that didn't happen very often but worked out nicely on club meeting days if neither of them had a sitting job.

"Hi, Dawn!"

I jumped at the voice. "Oh, Claud. You scared me. I was off in outer space."

"Well, land your vehicle," she replied. "I'm here now."

"How are the Newtons?" I asked.

"Fine, except Lucy has a cold."

"Isn't *any*one well around here?"

"You and I are," Claudia pointed out.

"Oh, yeah. I guess I was thinking of the Pikes."

Jessi arrived then and settled herself on the floor. "Gosh, I miss Mal," she said. "We haven't even been able to talk on the phone much. And I can't go visit her because Squirt hasn't had the chicken pox yet and Mama doesn't want him to get them when he's so young. I don't see how he could catch them from *me* if I don't have them, but Mama is being extra careful."

We sympathized with Jessi while the others arrived (except for Mal, of course). I watched Mary Anne and Kristy come in. They'd been giggling on the way upstairs, but they stopped when they entered BSC headquarters. They headed for their usual spots.

"Hi," I said to Mary Anne as she flopped down on the bed.

"Hi." Mary Anne barely looked at me.

I was about to ask her if she and Kristy had had fun, when Kristy tapped her pencil on the arm of the director's chair. Then she stuck the pencil over one ear. "Please come to order," she said loudly. "Treasurer?"

Stacey stood up and opened the treasury envelope. "Dues day!" she announced.

"*Oh,*" we all groaned. But we obediently reached for our money.

Stacey collected it and then dropped her own dues in. "Money, money, money," she said with a sigh.

I glanced at Mary Anne, almost laughing. Mary Anne couldn't help smiling back, but she looked as if the effort pained her.

"Anybody need money for anything?" asked Kristy. "It sounds as if we're loaded."

Stacey made a face. If she had her way, the treasury would just keep growing fatter and fatter and fatter. . . .

"I could use another drawing pad for my Kid-Kit," said Jessi.

"Well, I hate to admit it, but I need another box of watercolors," said Stacey. "Charlotte is turning into an artist. She paints almost as much as she reads, these days."

"Hey, guess what I noticed when Charlie was dropping us off here this afternoon," spoke up Mary Anne, but at that moment, the phone rang.

"First job call of the week!" cried Kristy. "I just love the first call. It's sort of an adventure. Who'll be on the other end? What — " Then Kristy realized she better answer the phone. "Hello, Baby-sitters club," she said.

Kristy listened for awhile, and then Mary Anne set up a job for Stacey with Nina and Eleanor Marshall.

"All right, so guess what I noticed," said Mary Anne as soon as the business had been taken care of.

"What?" said everybody but Kristy. I figured she knew already, and I wondered why I felt so left out, since no one else knew.

"The 'For Sale' sign is down in front of my old house."

"You're kidding!" exclaimed Claudia, jumping up to look out her window. "It was there this morning. . . . Yup, it's gone."

"Something must have happened today," I said. "I guess we'll hear all about it at dinner tonight. Right, sis?"

Mary Anne paused. "Right," she said finally.

"Are you having trouble selling your house?" Stacey asked Mary Anne.

"I don't know," she replied. "I mean, I guess if it's up for sale for a long time, then Dad will consider that trouble. But it hasn't been up too long yet. I'm dying to find out what happened today."

"Maybe a family full of cute guys will move in," said Claudia.

Kristy made a face. "How about a family full of *kids?*"

"Don't we have enough kids to sit for now?" I asked.

"We can never have too many," said Mary Anne shortly.

"I was just *kidding*," I told her.

"Oh."

We stopped our discussion then to take a series of phone calls. We lined up jobs with the Rodowskys and with Charlotte Johanssen. The third call was for a job with Jenny Prezzioso.

Both Mary Anne and I were free.

Uh-oh, here we go again, I thought.

But Mary Anne just said sweetly to me, "You take it, Dawn."

I looked at her in surprise. Had Kristy had a talk with her that afternoon?

"Me? You're going to let *me* take it?" I exclaimed.

"Sure." Mary Anne penciled my name into the book.

"Wait a sec," I said slowly. "You're just letting me have the job because you don't like taking care of Jenny, right?" (Jenny is a real brat. Mary Anne is actually more tolerant of her than the rest of us are, but she had sat for Jenny twice recently, and even Mary Anne has her limits.)

"No, I'm — " Mary Anne began to protest. But we all knew that whatever she was about to say would be a big, fat lie.

I watched Mary Anne's face closely. Was she trying to hide a smile?

"You are the worst liar!" I exclaimed.

"I know!" Mary Anne began to laugh.

Everyone else laughed, too. The tension seemed to break between my sister and me.

"Are you sure you want to give up a perfectly good job?" I asked.

"With Jenny? Are you kidding, sis? Of course I do."

More laughter. I began to relax.

The phone rang twice. Once it was Kristy's brother Sam saying, "Is this Al-Jon's Pizza? I'd like two large pies with everything." We know enough now to ignore any weird call we get. It's always Sam. He's an incurable joker.

"GOOD-BYE . . . *SAM!*" yelled Kristy when Sam had finished giving his pizza order.

"Jessi?" spoke up Stacey.

"Yeah?" Jessi looked sort of alone on the floor, but I knew it was very possible to look alone and not feel alone, or to be with a whole group of people and feel like no one is alive except you. I suspected that Jessi felt fine.

"Have you spoken to Mal lately?" asked Stacey.

"Last night. And guess what. Now Claire and Margo aren't feeling too good."

"Well, that's it," said Stacey.

"That's what?" Kristy wanted to know.

"That's all eight kids. They're *all* sick. Just what Mrs. Pike was afraid of. What's wrong with Claire and Margo?" Stacey asked Jessi. "The triplets' pneumonia?"

"Mal didn't think so," Jessi answered. "She

said they sounded more as if they just had colds."

"Let's hope so, for Mr. and Mrs. Pike's sakes," I said.

"Claire and Margo weren't even going to stay home from school today," added Jessi.

"I guess that's something," said Stacey. "I used to make my mother crazy when I stayed home sick . . . *me*. One person. Can you imagine waiting on *six* sick kids? Well, Nicky and Vanessa aren't actually sick, but still . . ."

The meeting was almost over. The numbers on Claud's digital clock were creeping toward six. At 5:59, since we weren't on a job call, Mary Anne felt it was safe to ask Kristy a nonbusiness question.

"What are you doing next Sunday?" she wanted to know.

"Nothing. Why? Are you free?"

Mary Anne nodded.

- "You want to come over? Better yet, come for dinner on Saturday and spend the night. I'm sure it'll be okay with Mom. Karen and Andrew will be there, and our house will be so crazy no one will notice another person."

"Great!" replied Mary Anne. "Thanks! I'm there."

I should have been happy, considering how I'd been complaining about the weekends and being with Mary Anne. I knew that. But I wasn't happy. Not one bit. I felt left out, which I knew was silly. If Mary Anne and I *hadn't* been sisters Kristy probably wouldn't have asked me, either. But that wasn't the problem. What was bothering me was that Mary Anne had started this. *She* had asked if *Kristy* was free. Maybe she didn't like the weekends any better than I did. And if that were true, what did it say about us? I was beginning to wonder if we were meant to be sisters at all.

CHAPTER 11

Even though I was hurt, I made a special effort to be nice to Mary Anne that night. And she seemed like her regular old self. On our way home, she teased me about the job with Jenny. Later, when I grew quiet, she asked, "Is anything wrong?"

"Oh, no. I'm fine," I said quickly. "Looking forward to sitting for Jenny."

Mary Anne giggled.

We were riding our bicycles through what was left of the late afternoon sun. Soon it would be dark.

"Have you spoken to Jeff lately?" asked Mary Anne.

I smiled. Mary Anne knows that talking to Jeff usually cheers me up. "Yeah. He's fine." I paused. Should I tell Mary Anne about Dad's girlfriend? Yes, I decided. She was my best friend and my sister. She should know about things like that. "Um, my dad's got a girlfriend who's over at the house all the time. At least, that was what Jeff said."

"Does Jeff like her?" Mary Anne wanted to know.

"Mmm. . . ." I frowned. "It was hard to tell. I think he's trying to like her."

Mary Anne accepted that.

We reached our house, put our bicycles in the barn, and ran inside. All during dinner that evening I was nice to Mary Anne. She was nice back. Maybe we were getting along better after all.

I hoped so.

Mary Anne remembered to ask her father about their old house, but all Richard said was, "The real estate broker told me she thought she had a buyer for the house, but she didn't give me any more details."

Pretty boring.

When dinner was over and the kitchen had been cleaned up (in jiffy time, thanks to Richard's help), Mary Anne and I headed upstairs to do our homework.

"What have you got?" Mary Anne asked as we settled down at our desks. They were right next to each other.

I made a face. "Math and science," I replied. "And a little English."

"And I've got math and science, too, plus French. I am really going to have to concentrate," added Mary Anne. "This math is hard."

"Definitely," I agreed.

We opened our books and worked silently. When it had taken fifteen minutes for me to solve the first problem, and Mary Anne had solved three, I realized I wasn't concentrating very well. The room was too quiet. I needed some music to help me pay attention.

I reached over and turned on my radio. I keep it tuned to WSTO, the local station, all year long in case of a surprise school closing. WSTO usually doesn't have very good music, though, so I steeled myself for a polka festival or something. Instead, I found the WSTO Fifties Festival.

"Oh, great!" I exclaimed. "I don't believe it. WSTO never has good music like this. . . . What is this song? . . . Oh, it's Buddy Holly — I think."

Mary Anne tossed me a funny look, but I was so caught up in the music that I barely paid attention to her. I listened to the end of the song, the music turned down low, and to the beginning of the next one before I went back to work. The music did the trick. I solved four problems quickly and I knew they were right.

But . . . "Dawn?" spoke up Mary Anne in the middle of an Elvis Presley song.

"Yeah?"

"Could you please turn that off?"

"Why? Don't you like the music?"

"No. I mean — no, it's not that. I just can't concentrate."

I sighed. I turned the radio lower, but not off.

We worked for about five more minutes before Mary Anne said tensely, "Dawn, I really need you to turn that *off*. I can't think unless I have silence."

Without a word I switched the radio off.

"Thank you," said Mary Anne.

"You're welcome," I replied. (But not really, I thought.)

We worked for another five minutes — until I realized something. I *wasn't* working. I needed the music. I don't always need music, but that night I did.

I turned the radio back on.

"Dawn!" exclaimed Mary Anne.

"What?"

"The radio. I just told you I can't work with that noise."

"And tonight I can't work without it."

"Can't you please turn it off?"

"*No.* Go in the guest room and work there if it bothers you so much."

"*Me?* Go in the *guest* room?"

"Yeah. Nothing in there is going to bite you." And then I added, "The secret passage is in *here*."

Mary Anne bristled. "I'm not afraid of that stupid passage. Besides, being afraid doesn't have anything to do with anything. The point is, you're throwing me out of our room."

"I am not throwing you out!" I cried.

"Well, you were the one who wanted me to share your room so badly. And now you're telling me to do my homework in another room!"

"Just for to*night!*" I shouted.

"But my desk is in *here* — where you insisted it be."

"You went along with it."

"So?"

"So it's not my fault your desk is in here. And it's not my fault you can't concentrate without absolute silence."

"I am — " Mary Anne was exploding when we both saw Tigger jump off of her bed and streak out of the room.

I don't know about Mary Anne, but that was when I realized just how loud our fighting had become. And wouldn't you know, about three seconds later Mom and Richard ran into our room.

"All right," said Richard, "what's going on in here?"

He and Mom were standing just inside the doorway, looking from me to Mary Anne and back again. They were waiting for an answer.

Mary Anne pointed to me. "*She* is being too noisy," she told her father. "I can't concentrate on my homework."

I pointed at Mary Anne. "*She* wants total silence," I told my mother. "*I* can't concentrate on *my* homework that way."

"What kind of noise are you making?" Mom asked me.

"I've just got the radio on. WSTO is having a Fifties Festival."

"I'd go work in the guest room, but my desk is in here," said Mary Anne pointedly.

"Wait a second," said Mom. "Nobody should have to leave."

"Well, someone's going to have to," I replied.

Mom's face immediately took on that "Now-listen-to-me-young-lady" look.

"Now listen to me, young lady," she said. (I knew it! She was mad, all right. I don't get called "young lady" very often.) "I don't want to hear any talking back."

"Mom, I — "

"All right, wait a second," Richard broke in. "This is getting us nowhere. Let's start at the beginning. Sharon and I need to hear the whole story. Dawn, will you please tell your side?"

I smirked. Mary Anne's father wanted to hear my side first, not his own daughter's.

"Okay," I said. "We both have a lot of homework tonight, right?" I gave Mary Anne a chance to talk, hoping that would make me look good.

"Right," she said sulkily.

"And we both agreed that we need to concentrate, right?" I was being *awfully* fair.

"Right."

"Okay. We started working and I couldn't get the math. The room was *too* quiet. So I turned on the radio to help me concentrate.

And right away I could work better. Only the next thing I knew, Mary Anne was fighting with me."

"I was not!" she cried.

"Never mind," said her father. "Okay, now tell us your side from the beginning, Mary Anne."

Mary Anne drew in her breath. "It was just like Dawn said. Only the radio was driving me crazy. I need quiet to work in."

"Couldn't you give in just a little?" Richard asked Mary Anne. "Try something new. I don't think you're being fair to Dawn."

And *I* couldn't believe that *Richard* was speaking. Richard, King of the Rules. Richard, who used to make Mary Anne wear her hair in braids, who wouldn't let her talk on the phone after dinner or ride her bike downtown. The King of the Rules was telling Mary Anne to give in a little, and was taking my side. What a surprise!

But I had another surprise coming, because just then Mom said, "Richard, don't be tough on Mary Anne. If she needs silence for her homework then she needs silence. Don't expect her to change. Besides, I don't think the girls should be working and listening to music at the same time."

What? It sounded almost as if my mom were making a rule. Worse than that, though, Mom was taking Mary Anne's side.

I challenged her. "So? What are you guys going to do about this? I want music and Mary Anne doesn't. What are you going to do?" I glanced at Mary Anne. Darn her. She was just sitting there crying. Now she would get attention and sympathy from Mom and Richard.

Wrong again. She only got it from Mom. The room was divided into camps. Mom and Mary Anne *versus* Richard and me. We were even standing on different sides, facing each other.

"The easy solution to this," said Richard, "is for the girls to do their homework in separate rooms."

"But who's going to leave?" asked Mom. "Whoever leaves is going to feel as if she's been kicked out." She put her hands on Mary Anne's shoulders. Mary Anne just kept on crying.

"Maybe the girls could alternate," suggested Richard.

"You know," I said to Mary Anne, "when my *real* brother was living here, we hardly ever fought like this. In fact, you and I didn't fight until you moved in."

105

"Until we became *step*sisters," said Mary Anne angrily.

"Okay, okay, that's enough," said Richard. "Do you girls think you can work this problem out tonight?"

"Yes," I said. "I'll work in the stupid guest room."

"Don't bother," replied Mary Anne. "It would be silly for you to do that since I'm going to be sleeping there tonight." And with that, she started yanking the covers off of her bed.

Mom gave me a look that plainly said, "*Now* see what you've done?"

But I didn't care. Mary Anne was just as much a part of this problem as I was. If she wanted to go and sleep in the guest room — fine. That was her decision. She sure was making me look bad, though. I had not, I realized, gotten just a stepsister. I'd gotten a wicked stepsister.

CHAPTER 12

Saturday

Oh, wow, what a day. I've never been on a job quite like this one.

I know. I've never baby-sat for grown-ups — or for Mallory! (Well, we didn't really have to sit for her.)

Be careful what you say. Sometime she might have to sit for you.

Never! Okay, Kristy. Let's write this job up.

All right. I'll start. We sat at the Pikes' today. If you can believe it, every single person in that family is now either sick or injured.

Well, let's be fair. Mallory, Nicky, and Vanessa are much better. They'll *all be in school on monday.*

Right. But Margo and Claire are sick now. Their colds turned into bronchitis. And Mrs. Pike injured her knee playing tennis, which left Mr. Pike to take care of everyone, so he tried to cook dinner last night and he wound up burning not only the food, but his hand....

A Pike nightmare! In all honesty, nobody was in *dire* straits that Saturday. As Jessi pointed out, Mal, Nicky, and Vanessa were just about better, except that Nicky would have to wear his cast for two more weeks. And the triplets were on the road to recovery, but they needed their rest because they still tired out very quickly. Margo and Claire were feeling the worst of all, Mrs. Pike wasn't in much pain but she couldn't walk, and Mr. Pike was in more pain and couldn't use his right hand.

All in all, it was not a healthy household, and with both the adults out of commission, Mrs. Pike thought they could use some help. So on Saturday morning (after Mr. Pike had spent half the night waiting around in the emergency room), Mrs. Pike called Claudia to see if the BSC could provide two sitters on an emergency basis (extra pay) for most of the day. Claudia couldn't take the job, but she called the other club members and found that Jessi and Kristy were free for the day. So Charlie drove Kristy to the Ramseys', picked up Jessi, and then dropped the girls off at the Pikes'.

"Thanks!" they called as he backed down the driveway, and Kristy added, "I'll call you later about a ride home!"

Jessi rang the Pikes' bell then, and both she and Kristy were surprised when Mallory answered the door. She was even dressed.

"You're up!" exclaimed Jessi.

"Yup," said Mal. "Out of bed. I even feel pretty good, but I am *not* up to handling this crowd today. Not by myself. The three of us ought to be able to handle things, though, with a little help from Nicky and Vanessa. We'll be going back to school on Monday."

"Great!" said Kristy. She started to let herself in, but Mal held the door closed.

"Wait a sec," she said. She turned and walked away. Jessi and Kristy looked at each other with question marks on their faces. "Okay," said Mal, returning. She opened the door a crack and stuck her hand out. In it were two surgeon's masks. "Wear these whenever you're in the house," she said. "They'll keep you from catching pneumonia or bronchitis — I hope."

"Do we *have* to?" asked Kristy.

"Do you want pneumonia?" replied Mal.

"Let me think it over," said Kristy. "I could use a break from school." But, of course, she put her mask on. So did Jessi.

Then Mal let them in.

"Oh, my lord," said Kristy, sounding just like Claudia. "What a mess. I know what our first job is."

The Pike house looked, as Richard would say, as if a tornado had blown through it. There was stuff everywhere. And no one had cleaned up the kitchen from the disastrous dinner the night before.

"Well, you might think you know what your first job is," Mal told Kristy and Jessi, "but the clean-up will have to come later. Guess what comes first — breakfast."

"*Break*fast?" repeated Kristy. "For everyone?"

"Yup. And seven of those breakfasts have to be served in bed on trays."

According to Jessi, Kristy looked, at that moment, as if she were going to faint. But she pulled herself together. "Okay. Breakfast. What do people like to eat?"

"Oh, don't ask them," replied Mal. "You'll get ten different answers. Breakfast this morning is scrambled eggs, toast, and orange juice. For *every*body. Oh, and coffee for Mom and Dad."

"All right," said Kristy uncertainly.

And Jessi added, "I thought Claire didn't like scrambled eggs."

"She doesn't," replied Mal. "But don't worry about it."

So my friends set to work in the kitchen. As it turned out, they had to clean it up just a little bit in order to use it. When that was done they set up an assembly line to fix the breakfasts. Mal scrambled a dozen and a half eggs in two huge frying pans. Jessi made toast after piece of toast, and Kristy set seven trays, plus three places at the table.

"Oh, set two more places," said Mal. "For you and Jessi."

"That's okay," Kristy replied. "I don't think we're going to be eating much. I think we'll be pretty busy."

Kristy was right. No sooner had the girls started carrying the trays upstairs than they heard comments such as, "But I don't *like* scrambled eggs," or, "I want *French* toast, not regular toast," or "Can't I have milk instead of orange juice?"

"This is NOT a restaurant," Mal yelled from the hallway, where everyone could hear her. "Either eat it or beat it."

"We can't beat it," said Claire pathetically. "We have to stay id our beds. Bobby said dot to get up."

"Bobby?" Jessi asked Mal.

"She means Mommy."

Kristy, Mal, and Jessi finished passing out the unwelcome trays. The only people who seemed glad to see them were Mr. and Mrs. Pike. Then Mal sat down to breakfast with Vanessa and Nicky.

Kristy and Jessi took coffee to Mal's parents. They brought paper towels to Claire, who had spilled orange juice over her quilt. Then Margo said, "Could I puh-*lease* have sub fruit?"

"Some fruit?" repeated Jessi. "I don't see why not. That's healthy."

So Jessi sliced up a banana for Margo.

"You'll be sorry," Mal warned her.

"Why?" asked Jessi.

She found out soon enough.

"If Margo gets a banana, then I want milk," said Byron.

"And I want fruit, too," said Adam.

"And I want French toast," said Jordan.

Breakfast wasn't over for two hours.

The day wore on. Kristy and Jessi did all the chores Mr. Pike had planned to do. They washed seven loads of laundry. They changed the triplets' beds. They emptied overflowing wastebaskets.

"Remind me," Kristy said as she and Jessi were folding the third load of laundry, "never to baby-sit on an emergency basis again. I'm not sure I could take it."

"But think of all the money we're earning," Jessi pointed out.

"I know. And just imagine — our parents do this for free everyday."

"They must be crazy."

Ding, ding, ding.

"Darn. There's Margo and Claire's bell again," said Kristy. "I'd like to kill Mal for giving it to them."

"I'll see what they want," said Jessi. She happily abandoned the laundry.

Jessi ran up to the girls' room. She checked

her mask before opening their door. It was in place.

"Yes?" she said.

Margo and Claire were both tucked into Margo's bed. They were giggling.

"Guess what we are," said Margo.

"Mmm, you're . . ." Jessi had no idea what they were.

"We're two peas in a pod!" shouted Claire.

Jessi giggled. "That's pretty funny. Who thought it up?"

"Be!" cried Claire.

"Be!" cried Margo.

Which was pretty funny itself, except that it caused an argument over who really had thought it up.

At four-thirty, Mal said to Jessi and Kristy, "We should start working on dinner. I'm a little nervous. We're running out of stuff."

"You're low on milk," said Jessi.

"I know. And on bread and butter and eggs. How are we going to last until Monday? That's when the doctor said Dad could start using his hand again."

"Maybe Stacey's mother could go to the store for you," suggested Jessi, "since she lives — "

"Wait!" cried Kristy. "I've got an idea. We'll

ask Charlie to stop at the store on his way over here. Can you pay him back for whatever he buys?"

"Sure," replied Mal.

So Kristy talked Charlie into doing the Pikes' shopping. She had to agree to pay him for his work, but that was okay. He deserved it. Especially since, after he reached the Pikes', he put on a surgeon's mask and stayed to help my friends cook dinner.

When the job was done, and he and Kristy and Jessi were walking to his car, Charlie said, "Boy, the Pikes' house sure is clean. Does it always look that way?"

Kristy and Jessi grinned at each other. If only he knew.

Charlie started the car, and at the last minute, Kristy realized that they might as well pick up Mary Anne for her overnight at the Brewer/Thomas mansion, since they were in our neighborhood.

That was fine with me. Mary Anne, my wicked stepsister, had been sleeping in the guest bedroom ever since Monday night, when we'd had our fight. She hadn't spoken to me, either, until that morning when she'd said she would be moving back in with me on Sunday when she returned from Kristy's.

115

Sleeping in one room and keeping her stuff in another room was too inconvenient, she'd said.

Well, tough. I'd decided I didn't want her sharing my room anymore.

CHAPTER 13

After Mary Anne went to Kristy's house that night, I had plenty of time to think about what happened after our fight on Monday. It had taken a long time for me to realize that Mary Anne and I were not meant to share a room. I'd wanted a sister so badly. Sisters, I'd thought, should share *every*thing — a room, their clothes, their secrets, even their germs. Just like Claire and Margo, or Mallory and Vanessa.

I think Mary Anne had felt the same way. Or she'd tried to.

But something was very wrong. I didn't want to admit it, but it was true. That was the first thing I'd thought when I'd awakened alone in my room on Tuesday morning. *Something is very wrong.*

In school that day, Mary Anne wouldn't speak to me. She doesn't get angry very often, but when she does, she's an expert with the silent treatment.

I wasn't surprised. I hadn't expected her to speak to me. Anyway, as long as *she* wasn't speaking to *me*, it was a good excuse for *me* not to speak to *her*. I did, however, decide to do something bold. I decided to talk to Kristy about my problem. But I also knew that Kristy was much better friends with Mary Anne than with me. I also knew that Kristy had been through a remarriage, a move into her stepfather's house, and the experience of gaining a stepbrother, a stepsister, and even an adopted sister. I figured she might be sympathetic. And I was right.

I caught up with Kristy at her locker before study hall. That was a good time to talk because it wouldn't matter much if we were late for study hall.

"Kristy?" I said.

Kristy was busy jamming stuff into her locker.

"Yeah? Oh, hi, Dawn."

"Hi. . . . I need to talk to you."

"I thought you might."

"You did?"

"Yup. I know what happened between you and Mary Anne last night."

x

118

"Oh."

"Listen, it's okay. I've been through just what you're going through, except that I never had to share a room with anyone."

Kristy and I talked all the way to study hall, and right through it until the end of the period. No one noticed or cared. Anyway, Kristy told me a lot of things that made sense. She said that it's hard for new families to fit together. Everyone tiptoes around, trying to figure everyone else out. People get mad. People feel threatened. They need their space. That's why her mother and Watson had been glad that all the kids could have their own rooms at Watson's big house.

Kristy also said that it wasn't unusual for parents to side with their stepchildren during arguments. "They just want their stepkids to like them. They're trying to make things work."

And then Kristy reminded me of the Arnold twins. "The girls needed separate rooms because they needed personal space."

Or emotional space, I thought, remembering my conversation with Jeff.

"Thanks, Kristy," I said, just before the bell rang. "I really appreciate this."

"No problem."

"I hope this doesn't insult you, but I thought you might not want to talk to me about this. I mean, because you're really, um, a little closer to Mary Anne than to me."

"Maybe," said Kristy, "but you guys are best friends, too. Or at least you were, and I'm sure you will be again someday. Anyway, I wouldn't want to see a great friendship dissolve, especially when my two good friends are part of it."

Well, no matter what else you say about Kristy, you have to admit that when the chips are down, she comes through. I'm not sure I would have been as nice to Kristy if she were having a fight with Mary Anne as she'd been to me that day.

When study hall was over, Kristy and I hugged each other.

I did some heavy thinking after school on Tuesday. It was a good time for it, since Mom and Richard were at work and Mary Anne was baby-sitting. I lay down on the bed in my room and looked around.

The room was so crowded you could barely walk through it. You had to edge around the beds and squeeze past the desks. The closet door only opened halfway because it was blocked by my armchair. There just wasn't any other spot for that chair.

I closed my eyes. I pictured the room the way it used to be, nice and light and airy and open. Now it was not only crowded, but messy. (Or as messy as Richard would let it get.) Since both Mary Anne and I are neat people, this wasn't really our fault. It was just that there was nowhere to put all of Mary Anne's stuff. The closet was overflowing, and things that we'd stashed under the beds sort of kept leaking out.

It occurred to me that living under those conditions would drive anyone crazy, but Mary Anne and I had other problems, too. The two of us and Mom and Richard really *were* struggling to fit together as a family. I pictured Richard making Mom breakfast every weekend, and Mom never eating half of it. I pictured Mom trying to cook dinner and clean for Richard, and never pleasing him. I pictured Mary Anne rushing Tigger into the kitchen and thinking she had to protect him from Mom after he'd gotten sick. And I pictured the fight Monday night — Richard and me facing off against Mom and Mary Anne. Each parent was siding with his or her stepkid. As Kristy had said, Richard just wanted me to like him, and

Mom just wanted Mary Anne to like her. What we really needed was for Mary Anne and me to like each other and to like living together.

That was hard, considering how differently Mary Anne and I had been raised. When we had just been friends our differences hadn't mattered so much, but now that we were trying to become a family, they mattered a lot.

I sighed. I knew that Mary Anne and I shouldn't be sharing a room. We needed our space, and anyway, sharing wasn't practical. But I had insisted that we share my room. Mary Anne had said so during our fight and she was right. I'd put pressure on her to share, even though she didn't really want to. So how could I admit that I'd been wrong? Or did I even have to?

If I could help it, I didn't want to admit to that. I wanted Mary Anne to move out, but I didn't want her to think it had anything to do with her or me or our ability to share a room. I wanted her to move out for some other reason.

Hmm. Now what other reason could there be? Mary Anne could move out because . . . because . . . Not because the room was too messy. I'd said we could fit everything in just fine. Not because she didn't like my room, because I knew she did, or used to. Well, except for the secret passage, which she was afraid of.

Wait a second! The secret passage! Maybe I could use the passage to scare Mary Anne out of our room. That would solve everything. It would be understandable, and neither of us would have to admit that Mary Anne had left because we couldn't get along. Furthermore, I could take revenge on my stepsister without her knowing it. I could get back at her for all the stinky things she'd done — getting me in trouble with Mom, complaining about Mom's food, following Mom around with the Dustbuster, getting chummy with Kristy and leaving me out of things, catching Mom's bouquet, taking the job at the Perkinses', and pitying me for not having a boyfriend. I could watch Mary Anne panic, but no one would know I was the cause of the trouble. Not if I put on the horror show when Mom and Richard weren't around. They'd just think Mary Anne's imagination had run away with her. And they'd be delighted to see her move into the guest room.

Those were my thoughts on Tuesday, after I spoke to Kristy. For the rest of the week I planned my revenge. On Wednesday afternoon I sneaked into the secret passage. I had to be very quiet, since Mary Anne was at home. I checked the passage to make sure it was in the same shape as the last time I'd been in it, which was quite awhile ago. I also tried the secret door to my room. Everything seemed to be in order.

On Thursday I called Jeff. I needed his help.

"Hi," I said when he picked up the phone. "It's me."

"Hi, you. How are you doing?"

"Fine. How are you and Dad?"

"We're fine," replied Jeff. "What's up?"

"I need to scare Mary Anne."

"You need to what?"

"Scare Mary Anne," I repeated. I told Jeff about the plan I was forming.

"*Oh*," said Jeff knowingly. "Well, you could . . ."

And Jeff rattled off a list of things I could do that were sure to make Mary Anne's hair stand on end.

By tonight — when it was time for Mary Anne's overnight with Kristy — I couldn't wait for her to leave. I needed the house to myself that night, and I would have it soon. I would be the only one home that evening, since Mom and Richard were going to a dinner party. I had some things to set up, and I needed everyone out of the house so I could enter and leave the secret passage without being seen, and so that I could test a few things.

I scheduled Operation: Scare Mary Anne for Monday night. On Monday night Mom and Richard would be at a PTO meeting at school. It was supposed to last from eight until nine-thirty, which meant that Mary Anne and I would be alone from about seven-thirty until ten. However, as far as Mary Anne knew, I would not be at home. I would be at the Pikes', where I'd suddenly been called to help Mallory with her sick and injured family. I just hoped Mary Anne wouldn't try to call me there, because of course, I wouldn't be there. I would be in the secret passage, if all went as planned.

Anyway, I was pretty glad when Charlie Thomas pulled up to our house in that broken-down car of his. I ran outside even before Mary Anne did.

"Hi, Kristy! Hi, Jessi!" I said. "Hi, Sam."

"Hi, Dawn," they replied, and Kristy added, "Is Mary Anne ready?"

"Almost. She'll be here in just a sec."

A few moments later, Mary Anne dashed outside.

She climbed into the car.

She didn't say a word to me.

So when everyone else called out, " 'Bye, Dawn!" I pointedly replied, " 'Bye, *Mary Anne*," and secretly thought, "You wicked stepsister, you."

CHAPTER 14

These were Jeff's ideas for Operation: Scare Mary Anne —

    1. Pretend to be a ghost in the passage. (That was easy, since I'd done it before. I'd pretend to be the ghost of Jared Mullray.)

    2. After you've pretended to be a ghost and made a lot of noise, ring the doorbell and run away.

    3. While Mary Anne is checking the door (and getting scared), run through the passage to your room and leave something weird on her desk.

    4. Repeat steps 2 and 3.

    5. Finish by slowly opening the door to the passage in your bedroom. Mary Anne will probably be scared away from your room forever.

It was a good plan. I have to give Jeff credit for that. From three thousand miles away, he had come up with a surefire scare tactic.

As soon as I had the house to myself on Saturday, I began collecting things to hide in the secret passage. I wanted to sound like a really good ghost. I didn't specifically have to sound like Jared Mullray, though. Mary Anne would jump to that conclusion all by herself.

Who's Jared Mullray? I guess I should tell you that if our passage really *is* haunted, it's haunted by the ghost of a man who is said to have disappeared in it ages ago. That man was Jared Mullray, and the townspeople thought he was crazy. I'll agree that some odd things have happened in our passage. I'll even agree that there might be a ghost. But if there is, I don't think he's mean and I'm not afraid of him. Otherwise I wouldn't go in the passage alone at night — or at any time.

On Saturday evening I collected a saw, a handful of acorns, a tape recorder, my haunted house sound-effects tape, and two other things. I made sure there were batteries in the recorder and that it worked properly. Then, carrying our big flashlight, I brought the things into the passage and left them there. Since no one else was at home, I could enter the passage through my bedroom, instead of going all the way out to the barn and in the other entrance.

I tested the rest of my equipment. It sounded *good*.

Okay, Monday night. Hurry up and come.

Sunday was one of the longest days I've ever lived through. It was endless. Monday was only a little better because of school and our BSC meeting. It wasn't until dinnertime that I got to put the first part of my plan into action.

We were eating in the den in front of the TV.

"Excuse me," I said, getting up with my empty plate as if I were going to have a second helping. (I had wolfed my dinner down.)

In the kitchen, I quickly put some more food on my plate.

Then I picked up our phone and dialed the operator.

"Hi," I said quietly. "Maybe you can help me. I think something's wrong with our phone. Can you call me back?" I gave the operator our number.

When the phone rang, I snatched it up. "Thanks," I told the operator. "I guess it's working okay after all."

I waited a few more moments before hanging up and returning to the den.

"Who was on the phone?" Richard asked immediately.

"That was Mallory," I said. "Her parents are kind of worn out this evening so I told her I'd come over. She doesn't need a sitter, she just needs *help*. My homework is almost done."

Nobody questioned this.

So I left my house at the same time Mom and Richard left for the meeting at school. I headed for the Pikes', then doubled back. I stood in the dark yard outside my bedroom window until I saw the light in my room go on. I waited five more minutes until I was pretty sure Mary Anne was at her desk and working.

Then I crept into our barn.

I found the flashlight that I had hidden under some hay. I turned it on, opened a trapdoor in the floor of the barn, and climbed down a ladder to the end of the tunnel. The tunnel travels underground to our house, then up a flight of stairs and through another sort of tunnel that runs between walls in our house and winds up, of course, at the hidden door to my room.

I crept along silently until I had climbed the stairs. There at the head of the stairs were the things I had collected on Saturday night. I decided to start off simply, with the acorns.

I threw one down the passage. It rattled along and stopped near the doorway.

I threw another one.

Rattle, rattle, rattle.

I put my ear to the wall and listened for Mary Anne, but I couldn't hear a thing. I wished desperately for a peephole so I could spy on her. For all I knew, she wasn't even in the room. Maybe the phone had rung or something.

I decided to take a chance.

I tiptoed all the way to the doorway and threw the rest of the acorns at the wall of the passage.

I heard Mary Anne gasp. I was sure of it.

Perfect. Time for the saw.

If you hold one of those floppy, old-fashioned saws by the handle and wobble the saw back and forth, it makes the *weirdest* sounds. With a little imagination, anyone could think they were hearing a space creature . . . or a ghost.

I knew Mary Anne would hear Jared Mullray.

Then I put on the sound-effects tape. I had set it to play "The Howling Winds." When the winds died down, I turned the tape off. I knew Mary Anne was good and scared.

Okay. Time to ring the doorbell.

As quietly as I could, I left the passage, ran across the yard to our front door, rang the bell, then dashed back to the barn and through the passage again. At great risk, I opened the door into my room. I was holding a secret something that I had found on Saturday. It was a very realistic-looking silk rose. I laid it on top of Mary Anne's homework, then made a run for the passage.

Not a moment too soon. I could hear Mary Anne's footsteps on the stairs. I stayed in the passage with an ear to the door, but I didn't have to be nearby in order to hear Mary Anne's scream.

"Aughhh!"

She nearly scared *me*, and *I* knew why she was screaming.

I took my time leaving the passage. I wanted at least ten to fifteen minutes to go by before I rang the bell again. I even hung out in the barn for a few minutes. At last it was time to dash across the yard, ring the bell, and then run back through the passage. When I reached the door to my room I opened it cautiously, scrambled through, and laid a dried-out chicken bone on Mary Anne's notebook. It looked sort of like a human finger bone.

This time I didn't have to fly back into the passage. I could hear Mary Anne on the phone downstairs. She was asking for Logan. So I tiptoed into the passage, making sure the door didn't quite latch behind me.

It seemed like ages before Mary Anne dared to return to our room. When she did, I plastered myself against the wall in the passage. Before I could even start to crack the door open —

"Aughhh!"

Mary Anne saw the bone and let out a shriek. Then she must have seen the door to the passage, which I slowly pushed inward. I couldn't have opened it more than two inches when Mary Anne shrieked again and pounded down the stairs.

I decided that Operation: Scare Mary Anne was over.

I crept into our room, retrieved the rose and the bone, left them in the passage, then ran through it to the barn and across our yard, and let myself in the front door.

"Mary Anne?" I called.

"Aughhh!" she shrieked again.

"Aughhh!" I shrieked. "You scared me!" (She really had. She had jumped out of the living room just as I'd entered the house.)

Mary Anne was clutching Tigger and breathing heavily. "You won't believe what happened!" she exclaimed, and then proceeded to tell me everything. "That passage is *haunted*," she wound up, "just like I thought. . . . Hey, what are you doing home so early?"

"The passage is *not* haunted," I told her. "And I'm home because the Pikes were all tired and wanted to go to bed, so they didn't need me anymore."

"Oh," said Mary Anne. "But listen, that passage *is* haunted. I have never been so terrified. I even tried to call Logan. He wasn't home, though. Dawn, I can't spend another night in your room. I don't know how you can sleep in there, knowing the spirit of Jared Mullray is lurking around. I don't know how *I* slept in there. But I'm not going to do it anymore. I'm going to move into the guest room. Claudia said she would help me redecorate it if I ever wanted to."

"But, Mary Anne — " I began.

"I'm sorry," she said. "Do you know what

134

Jared did? First he tried to be really nice to me by leaving me a rose. Then he left me a *bone*. An old, dried-up finger bone. Isn't that sinister?"

"He left them?" I repeated. "Where?"

"Come on upstairs." Mary Anne led me to my room. "See? They're right — " Mary Anne stopped. "Where are they?" She looked toward the door to the secret passage, but it was securely closed. If you didn't know it was there, you'd never even notice it. "Well, they *were* here," said Mary Anne.

"Sure they were," I said soothingly.

"No, *really*. They were. Anyway, this is just more proof. Jared took them back. Dawn, I swear, I can't be in this room. At least not at night. Will you help me move my stuff into the guest room?"

"Of course," I replied.

Mary Anne and I began lugging her furniture into the other room. It wasn't easy, but we worked quickly anyway. And every now and then, as we were hefting up a chair or dragging her desk through the hall, we would look at each other and smile.

We smiled because we were both relieved — and not just that the "haunting" was over. We were relieved that we were each going to get our own space without having to admit that we couldn't share a room. I was sorry I'd scared Mary Anne so badly, but I knew I'd done the right thing. And when Mom and Richard came home they would convince Mary Anne that there was no ghost, and that her imagination was just working overtime. Eventually, she would believe them and forget the whole incident.

When most of Mary Anne's stuff had been moved out of my room, I said, "Mary Anne, I've got something for you."

It was my "now-we're-sisters" present, which I had bought and had been saving until Mary Anne and I *felt* more like sisters. It was a little pin in the shape of a cat. I knew Mary Anne had seen one once and liked it.

Of course, Mary Anne cried when she opened it. But that was okay. I wouldn't expect anything else from my sister.

CHAPTER 15

"Claudia, for heaven's sake. What are you doing?" I exclaimed.

It was 5:20 on a Friday afternoon. Mary Anne and I had just arrived at BSC headquarters for a meeting. Claudia was the only other person there. She was standing on her head, leaning against the wall. Her face was beet-red.

"I'm trying to get smarter," she said.

At least I was pretty sure that was what she'd said. It was hard to understand her with her long hair puddled around her head.

"You're trying to get *smarter*?" repeated Mary Anne incredulously.

"Mm-hmm. I heard that if you stand on your head, all your blood rushes to your brain and feeds the cells there. I figure I need all the brain food I can get. I have an English test tomorrow."

"Don't you think studying would help?" I asked.

Mary Anne nudged me. We were having trouble keeping straight faces.

From behind us a third voice spoke up. It was Kristy, who had just arrived. "I wonder . . ." she said tantalizingly.

I just knew she was waiting for someone to ask her what she was wondering about. So I obliged her. "What do you wonder?" I asked.

"Well, I've spent nearly all day sitting down," she replied, "so you can imagine where my blood has settled. I must have the smartest — "

"Kristy!" shrieked Mary Anne, and we began to laugh.

Claudia laughed so hard she fell over. When she stood up, she swayed back and forth a little.

"Are you okay?" I asked.

"I'm fine. Just light-headed. Is this how it feels to be a genius?"

"NO!" shouted Janine from her room.

Claudia rolled her eyes. Then she began rooting around her room — under her bed, under chairs, in boxes, in her desk drawer. At last she came up with a bag of Tootsie Rolls and a box of pretzel sticks.

We settled into our usual places. Kristy put on her visor and stuck the pencil over her ear. We ate and talked. At 5:25 Jessi and Mal arrived, and at 5:29, Stacey ran in.

"Oh, goody," said Kristy. "We're all here."

"But we still have one minute before the meeting starts," said Mary Anne, "and I would like to say that — "

"Five-thirty!" cried Kristy as Claud's digital clock changed. "Come to order, please, everyone!"

"Darn," said Mary Anne.

"Don't worry," Kristy told her. "As soon as the official business is over, you can tell us whatever it is — as long as we're between phone calls."

"Okay," said Mary Anne.

Mary Anne and I were sitting next to each other on Claud's bed. It had been four days since I had scared her with the ghost of Jared Mullray. Mary Anne had been sleeping in the guest room ever since. Also, we had been getting along better ever since. It wasn't like the time Mary Anne had slept in the guest room and not spoken to me. When she had moved out then she'd been angry. This time she'd moved out because of the secret passage. Also, all of her belongings were in the guest room, so it didn't feel like the guest room anymore. It felt like her own room. Furthermore, everyone — Mom, Richard, Mary Anne, and I — had been making an effort to work things out better.

One night, much to my surprise, Richard had said stiffly at dinner, "Ahem, ahem. . . . I have a suggestion."

"What is it?" asked Mom. She looked puzzled.

"I've been thinking about . . . about how the four of us have been getting along lately."

Immediately, Mary Anne and I stared at our hands. While she and I didn't squabble over the room anymore, we'd had a few other squabbles — with each other, with Mom, with Richard. And Mom and Richard were having their share of squabbles. Most of the arguing was over cleaning, cooking, and how neat or messy the house was.

"I propose," Richard went on, "that we make a list of the chores that need to get done around here, decide who's going to do what when, enter those things on a chart — and *stick to the chart*."

Mary Anne and I looked at Mom to see her reaction. Keeping a chore chart was completely against her nature, so I was pretty surprised when she said, "Okay, I agree. But I have something to say about meals in this house."

"Fair enough," said Richard.

"*I* propose," Mom began, "that each weekend, Dawn and I will cook the kinds of foods we like — enough for a week — and you and Mary Anne will cook the kinds of foods you like — enough for a week. Then at dinner each night there won't be any more forcing you to eat tofu or us to eat meat. Ordinarily, I don't like the idea of two different menus for one meal, but I don't see any way around this. Our eating habits are radically different and no one wants to change."

Richard looked at Mary Anne.

I looked at Mom.

"Okay," said Richard, Mary Anne, and I at once.

"Good," said Mom in a businesslike way, but I could see she was pleased.

"I — I have one more suggestion," I spoke up timidly. I couldn't believe what I was about to say.

"Yes?" said Mom encouragingly.

"I think we should all be more honest with each other. We should stop trying to please each other so much. We're going along with

141

things we don't like or believe in, or with things that annoy us — just to please each other. And it isn't working."

"What do you mean?" asked Richard gently.

"I mean, well, Mom *hates* bacon, Richard, but you always serve it to her at breakfast and she always says she likes what you serve. And Mary Anne, you can't stand the way my mom cleans, but instead of telling that to her, you just clean up after her. And I knew, and so did Mary Anne, that we shouldn't be sharing a room. But we kept forcing ourselves to try to make it work." (I almost let the cat out of the bag about the ghost just then, but luckily, I kept my mouth shut. Mary Anne would be mortified if she knew what I'd done, and I didn't want to hurt her.)

Anyway, after my outburst we were quiet for a moment or two. Then Richard said slowly, "You know, I think that's a good idea."

"Are you sure you aren't just saying that to please me?" I teased.

Richard laughed. Then Mom and Mary Anne laughed, too, and finally I joined in. Thank goodness, I thought. What if Richard hadn't taken that as a joke?

After that evening, things got better quickly. We really did make up a list of chores (and we stuck to it), and we really did start being more honest with each other.

"Dawn? Dawn?"

I shook myself. I'd been daydreaming — not a great thing to do during a club meeting. Kristy expects us to pay attention.

"Yes?" I said, frantically trying to figure out what had been going on.

"I *said*," said Mary Anne, "that Dad sold our old house, right?"

"Yup," I replied. "Well, almost. He signs the papers next week."

"Who's going to move in?" asked Kristy excitedly. "Future baby-sitting clients? That would be great."

"I think so," replied Mary Anne. "Dad said a family, didn't he, Dawn?"

I nodded.

"But he wasn't sure of the ages of the kids. He *did* say, though, that they're foreign."

"Foreign!" cried Stacey. "Oh, cool! Where are they from?"

Mary Anne and I glanced at each other.

"Austria?" I said. "The real estate agent was fuzzy on the details."

"Oh. Well, anyway, this is *really* exciting!" exclaimed Claudia.

"Yeah," agreed the rest of us.

"It would be fun to teach the kids English," added Jessi.

The phone rang then. It was Mrs. Pike needing two sitters for the following Saturday. After we'd lined up Mal and Stacey, I said, "So the Pike Plague is really over, Mal?"

"Yes," said Mallory with a sigh of relief. "Really and truly. All us kids are back in school, Mom's on her feet, and Dad can use his hand again. He's going to have a scar, though."

"Boy, you were lucky not to be left with any chicken pox scars," Kristy said to Mal. Then she added, "You *are* unscarred, aren't you?"

"For the most part," mumbled Mal, glancing at Jessi.

Jessi started to laugh.

"Okay," said Kristy. "Out with it. Where are your scars?"

"In unmentionable places," was all Mal would reply.

Not long after that, the meeting broke up. Mary Anne and I rode our bikes home. Mary

144

Anne was all excited because, just as the meeting had ended, Claud had said, "Mary Anne, we've got to start thinking about redoing your room. We've got to give it a little character. We've got to make your room say, 'Mary Anne Spier lives here.' "

" 'Mary Anne Spier lives here,' " Mary Anne repeated to me. "What would make the room say that?"

We talked about wallpaper and posters and throw rugs and things until we reached our house. Then we parked our bikes and headed inside.

"I wonder what Mom's doing home at this hour," I said as we passed her car in the driveway. "I hope nothing's wrong."

Nothing was. Mom had just finished up early at the office. But what a surprise Mary Anne and I had when we walked into the den after we'd called hi to her. We found Tigger curled up in her lap. He was purring loudly, his eyes half closed.

My mom was reading a book and looking a little sheepish.

"I don't believe it!" Mary Anne couldn't help saying.

I couldn't believe it, either.

"He just jumped up," Mom explained, "and he wouldn't go away. Before I knew it, he was asleep." She cleared her throat, then added, "I kind of like having him here."

And I, I thought, like having my new family here.

About the Author

ANN M. MARTIN did *a lot* of baby-sitting when she was growing up in Princeton, New Jersey. Now her favorite baby-sitting charge is her cat, Mouse, who lives with her in her Manhattan apartment.

Ann Martin's Apple Paperbacks are *Bummer Summer, Inside Out, Stage Fright, Me and Katie (the Pest)*, and all the other books in the Baby-sitters Club series.

She is a former editor of books for children, and was graduated from Smith College. She likes ice cream, the beach, and *I Love Lucy*; and she hates to cook.

Look for #32

KRISTY AND THE SECRET OF SUSAN

"Will Susan get better?" I asked.

"Maybe. Some educators and doctors believe that if an autistic child starts acquiring meaningful language by the time he's five, he can become much better. That hasn't happened for Susan."

Just when I was beginning to feel terribly sad, though, Mrs. Felder spoke again. "We're somewhat encouraged, her father and I," she said almost proudly, "because Susan is autistic but she's also a savant. That means she has some very specialized talents."

"Really?" I asked, intrigued.

"Yes. You should hear her play the piano. She's really remarkable," Mrs. Felder went on. "She astonishes everyone — her teachers, her doctors, even *music* teachers. She can usually play any new piece of music after hearing it only once. Just like that — she's got the whole thing memorized *and* she can play it."

148

Mrs. Felder paused. "But if you ask her how she is, what she wants for dinner, if she has to use the bathroom . . . nothing. No response. She never initiates conversations, either. She just does not communicate. She can be very trying at times, too. Stubborn. Especially if you want her to stop playing the piano. But she's never violent. . . . Do — do you still want the job?"

"Oh, yes!" I said. I guess you can tell by now that I was thoroughly fascinated with Susan. I'd never met anyone like her. I'd never even *heard* of anyone like her. I was also feeling just the teeniest bit angry, though. Susan was very special. That was obvious. But everyone treated her like some kind of outcast. Her parents were taking her out of one away-from-home school and putting her in another. Why couldn't they keep her with them? There are schools for handicapped kids around here. *Day* schools like the one Matt Braddock goes to in Stamford. Why didn't her parents try to help Susan make friends?

I decided that I would not only take on the job with Susan, but that I would use the month I had with her to show the Felders that she could live and learn and make friends *at home*. She did not have to be an outcast.

Read all the books
in the Baby-sitters Club series
by Ann M. Martin

1 *Kristy's Great Idea*
Kristy's great idea is to start *The Baby-sitters Club*!

2 *Claudia and the Phantom Phone Calls*
Someone mysterious is calling Claudia!

3 *The Truth About Stacey*
Stacey's different . . . and it's harder on her than anyone knows.

4 *Mary Anne Saves the Day*
Mary Anne is tired of being treated like a baby. It's time to take charge!

5 *Dawn and the Impossible Three*
Dawn thought she'd be baby-sitting — not *monster*-sitting!

6 *Kristy's Big Day*
Kristy's a baby-sitter — and a bridesmaid, too!

7 *Claudia and Mean Janine*
Claudia's big sister is super smart . . . and super *mean*.

8 *Boy-Crazy Stacey*
Stacey's too busy being *boy-crazy* to baby-sit!

\# 9 *The Ghost at Dawn's House*
Creaking stairs, a secret passage — there must be a ghost at Dawn's house!

\#10 *Logan Likes Mary Anne!*
Mary Anne has a crush on a *boy* baby-sitter!

\#11 *Kristy and the Snobs*
The kids in Kristy's new neighborhood are S-N-O-B-S!

\#12 *Claudia and the New Girl*
Claudia might give up the club — and it's all Ashley's fault!

\#13 *Good-bye Stacey, Good-bye*
Oh, no! Stacey McGill is moving back to New York!

\#14 *Hello, Mallory*
Is Mallory Pike good enough to join the club?

\#15 *Little Miss Stoneybrook . . . and Dawn*
Everyone in Stoneybrook has gone beauty-pageant crazy!

\#16 *Jessi's Secret Language*
Jessi's new charge is teaching her a *secret language*.

\#17 *Mary Anne's Bad-Luck Mystery*
Will Mary Anne's bad luck ever go away?

\#18 *Stacey's Mistake*
Has Stacey made a big mistake by inviting the Baby-sitters to New York City?

\#19 *Claudia and the Bad Joke*
Claudia is headed for trouble when she baby-sits for a practical joker.

#20 *Kristy and the Walking Disaster*
Can Kristy's Krushers beat Bart's Bashers?

#21 *Mallory and the Trouble with Twins*
Sitting for the Arnold twins is double trouble!

#22 *Jessi Ramsey, Pet-sitter*
Jessi has to baby-sit for a house full of . . . *pets!*

#23 *Dawn on the Coast*
Could Dawn be a California girl for good?

#24 *Kristy and the Mother's Day Surprise*
There are all *kinds* of surprises this Mother's Day.

#25 *Mary Anne and the Search for Tigger*
Tigger is missing! Has he been catnapped?

#26 *Claudia and the Sad Good-bye*
Claudia never thought she'd have to say good-bye to her grandmother.

#27 *Jessi and the Superbrat*
Jessi gets to baby-sit for a TV star!

#28 *Welcome Back, Stacey!*
Stacey's moving again . . . back to Stoneybrook!

#29 *Mallory and the Mystery Diary*
Only Mal can solve the mystery in the old diary.

#30 *Mary Anne and the Great Romance*
Mary Anne's father and Dawn's mother are getting *married!*

#31 *Dawn's Wicked Stepsister*
Dawn thought having a stepsister was going to be fun. Was she ever wrong!

#32 *Kristy and the Secret of Susan*
     Even Kristy can't learn all of Susan's secrets.

Super Specials:
1 *Baby-sitters on Board!*
     Guess who's going on a dream vacation? The Baby-sitters!

2 *Baby-sitters' Summer Vacation*
     Good-bye, Stoneybrook . . . hello, Camp Mohawk!

3 *Baby-sitters' Winter Vacation*
     The Baby-sitters are off for a week of winter fun!

THE BABY-SITTERS CLUB®

by Ann M. Martin

☐ MG43388-1	#1	Kristy's Great Idea	$3.25
☐ MG43387-3	#10	Logan Likes Mary Anne!	$3.25
☐ MG43660-0	#11	Kristy and the Snobs	$3.25
☐ MG43721-6	#12	Claudia and the New Girl	$3.25
☐ MG43386-5	#13	Good-bye Stacey, Good-bye	$3.25
☐ MG43385-7	#14	Hello, Mallory	$3.25
☐ MG43717-8	#15	Little Miss Stoneybrook...and Dawn	$3.25
☐ MG44234-1	#16	Jessi's Secret Language	$3.25
☐ MG43659-7	#17	Mary Anne's Bad-Luck Mystery	$3.25
☐ MG43718-6	#18	Stacey's Mistake	$3.25
☐ MG43510-8	#19	Claudia and the Bad Joke	$3.25
☐ MG43722-4	#20	Kristy and the Walking Disaster	$3.25
☐ MG43507-8	#21	Mallory and the Trouble with Twins	$3.25
☐ MG43658-9	#22	Jessi Ramsey, Pet-sitter	$3.25
☐ MG43900-6	#23	Dawn on the Coast	$3.25
☐ MG43506-X	#24	Kristy and the Mother's Day Surprise	$3.25
☐ MG43347-4	#25	Mary Anne and the Search for Tigger	$3.25
☐ MG42503-X	#26	Claudia and the Sad Good-bye	$3.25
☐ MG42502-1	#27	Jessi and the Superbrat	$3.25
☐ MG42501-3	#28	Welcome Back, Stacey!	$3.25
☐ MG42500-5	#29	Mallory and the Mystery Diary	$3.25
☐ MG42498-X	#30	Mary Anne and the Great Romance	$3.25
☐ MG42497-1	#31	Dawn's Wicked Stepsister	$3.25
☐ MG42496-3	#32	Kristy and the Secret of Susan	$3.25
☐ MG42495-5	#33	Claudia and the Great Search	$3.25
☐ MG42494-7	#34	Mary Anne and Too Many Boys	$3.25
☐ MG42508-0	#35	Stacey and the Mystery of Stoneybrook	$3.25
☐ MG43565-5	#36	Jessi's Baby-sitter	$3.25
☐ MG43566-3	#37	Dawn and the Older Boy	$3.25
☐ MG43567-1	#38	Kristy's Mystery Admirer	$3.25

More titles... ➡

The Baby-sitters Club titles continued...

❑ MG43568-X	#39 Poor Mallory!	$3.25
❑ MG44082-9	#40 Claudia and the Middle School Mystery	$3.25
❑ MG43570-1	#41 Mary Anne Versus Logan	$3.25
❑ MG44083-7	#42 Jessi and the Dance School Phantom	$3.25
❑ MG43572-8	#43 Stacey's Emergency	$3.25
❑ MG43573-6	#44 Dawn and the Big Sleepover	$3.25
❑ MG43574-4	#45 Kristy and the Baby Parade	$3.25
❑ MG43569-8	#46 Mary Anne Misses Logan	$3.25
❑ MG44971-0	#47 Mallory on Strike	$3.25
❑ MG43571-X	#48 Jessi's Wish	$3.25
❑ MG44970-2	#49 Claudia and the Genius of Elm Street	$3.25
❑ MG44969-9	#50 Dawn's Big Date	$3.25
❑ MG44968-0	#51 Stacey's Ex-Best Friend	$3.25
❑ MG44966-4	#52 Mary Anne + 2 Many Babies	$3.25
❑ MG44967-2	#53 Kristy for President	$3.25
❑ MG44965-6	#54 Mallory and the Dream Horse	$3.25
❑ MG44964-8	#55 Jessi's Gold Medal	$3.25
❑ MG45575-3	Logan's Story Special Edition Readers' Request	$3.25
❑ MG44240-6	Baby-sitters on Board! Super Special #1	$3.50
❑ MG44239-2	Baby-sitters' Summer Vacation Super Special #2	$3.50
❑ MG43973-1	Baby-sitters' Winter Vacation Super Special #3	$3.50
❑ MG42493-9	Baby-sitters' Island Adventure Super Special #4	$3.50
❑ MG43575-2	California Girls! Super Special #5	$3.50
❑ MG43576-0	New York, New York! Super Special #6	$3.50
❑ MG44963-X	Snowbound Super Special #7	$3.50
❑ MG44962-X	Baby-sitters at Shadow Lake Super Special #8	$3.50

Available wherever you buy books...or use this order form.

Scholastic Inc., P.O. Box 7502, 2931 E. McCarty Street, Jefferson City, MO 65102

Please send me the books I have checked above. I am enclosing $_____ (please add $2.00 to cover shipping and handling). Send check or money order - no cash or C.O.D.s please.

Name _____

Address _____

City_____ State/Zip _____

Please allow four to six weeks for delivery. Offer good in the U.S. only. Sorry, mail orders are not available to residents of Canada. Prices subject to change.

BSC1291

Don't miss out!

Join the BABY-SITTERS Fan Club!

Pssst... Know what? You can find out **everything** there is to know about *The Baby-sitters Club*. Join the BABY-SITTERS FAN CLUB! Get the hot news on the series, the inside scoop on all the Baby-sitters, and lots of baby-sitting fun...just for $4.95!

With your **two-year** membership, you get:

★ An official membership card!
★ A colorful banner!
★ The exclusive Baby-sitters Fan Club quarterly newsletter with baby-sitting tips, activities and more!

Just fill in the coupon below and mail with payment to:
THE BABY-SITTERS FAN CLUB,
Scholastic Inc., P.O. Box 7500, 2931 E. McCarty Street, Jefferson City, MO 65012.

- -

The Baby-sitters Fan Club

❑ **YES!** Enroll me in The Baby-sitters Fan Club! I've enclosed my check or money order (no cash please) for $4.95 made payable to Scholastic Inc.

Name _____ Age _____

Street _____

City _____ State/Zip _____

Where did you buy this *Baby-sitters Club* book?

❑ Bookstore   ❑ Drugstore   ❑ Supermarket   ❑ Book Club
❑ Book Fair   ❑ Other_____(specify)
Not available outside of U.S. and Canada.

BSC791